WITCH
Chocolate
BITES

BEWITCHED BY CHOCOLATE
MYSTERIES

BOOK FOUR

H.Y. HANNA

CONTENTS

CHAPTER ONE

"Over here, Caitlyn! This is a great spot!"

Caitlyn Le Fey followed her cousin, Pomona, across the wide green lawn which sloped down from the elegant Georgian façade of Huntingdon Manor. The space was already half-filled with families and couples sitting in small groups and she had to take care not to step on the various picnic blankets and cushions spread out across the grass. It was the opening night of the new Tillyhenge Open-Air Cinema and, from the number of people milling about, it looked like it was going to be a huge hit. This was the first time that such an event had been held in the local area and it seemed to have attracted residents from far and wide—as well as quite a few tourists—to the tiny Cotswolds village of Tillyhenge.

"Wow, look at all the people," said Pomona, turning her head to scan the area. She laughed. "I can't believe James was worried that locals wouldn't be into the idea. Like, who wouldn't wanna sit in the beautiful grounds of an English country manor on a balmy summer evening, enjoying a picnic and a movie?"

"I think James just didn't want to step on any toes," said Caitlyn. "When he inherited the title, a lot of the villagers were worried that he would introduce too many modern concepts. They were scared he'd destroy the heritage and traditions they were used to—you know, it's like the backbone to life on the estate."

"Yeah, but his ideas are making things better... like, breathing some life into the place!"

Caitlyn shrugged. "You know how people hate change, especially the older residents. Opening the Manor to the public and allowing tours was already a big step for them, so James wanted to go slowly." She smiled. "I think it's why his tenants love him so much—he's always putting their needs first and consulting them on everything."

Pomona gave Caitlyn a teasing sidelong glance. "Oooh, we're getting to know the new Lord Fitzroy very well, aren't we?"

Caitlyn felt a blush heat her cheeks and was annoyed with herself. "It's common knowledge that James Fitzroy is a fantastic landlord," she said quickly.

Pomona plunked the cushions they had brought with them down on the grass and made a face. "I wish we'd thought to bring more cushions. That grass looks a lot harder up close." She glanced enviously at a couple who were sitting on giant beanbags a few feet away. "Where did they get those from?" She scanned the crowd again, this time noting several couples and families who were also sitting on beanbags. "There's no way they *all* brought those from home!"

"I heard that James hired a company which provides beanbags for outdoor events... Look, they're there," said Caitlyn, pointing to a booth at the far side of the lawn. "Do you want me to grab us a couple?"

"Yeah, good idea," said Pomona, spreading out a blanket to face the giant screen erected at the end of the lawn. "I'll stay here and guard our spot."

Caitlyn made her way back across the lawn, passing a large poster of the movie being screened that evening. She grimaced as she saw the image of the muscled hero with a ridiculous mane of long, curly hair, brandishing a pistol and facing a tall, pale man in a black cloak, with fangs protruding from his mouth. Caitlyn sighed as she remembered that tonight's film was about Van Helsing, the legendary vampire hunter. She hadn't been keen on the movie, to be honest, but Pomona loved anything to do with the paranormal, and had insisted on coming.

Glancing at the groups with young children around her, Caitlyn reflected that a vampire movie seemed an odd choice for a family event. Then she looked at the poster again and realised that it was really a spoof horror movie, with the vampire looking more comical than scary. Still, she found the idea of the film distasteful and even a bit irritating.

Maybe it's because the supernatural isn't make-believe for me anymore—it's personal now, she thought ruefully. When she'd arrived in Tillyhenge two months ago and learned that she was descended from a long line of witches, Caitlyn suddenly found herself plunged into a strange new world, filled with magic and spells, myths and enchantments. Now, all the jokes and stereotypes about witches and vampires didn't seem so funny. In fact, she often found herself getting annoyed at the so-called "facts" about magic and the paranormal in the popular media—which were usually completely wrong.

As if echoing her thoughts, she heard a grumpy voice she recognised:

"What utter rubbish! This poster is an insult—an insult, do you hear me? It must be removed! Vampires do not sleep in coffins—nor do we lack reflections in mirrors. How do you suppose I shave in the mornings? And those fangs are far too long to be—"

Viktor!

Caitlyn hurried towards a small crowd gathering around a thin, balding old man, who was dressed in a black suit that looked like a relic from the last century. He was standing next to another poster of the movie, glowering at a teenage boy in a reflective vest, who'd obviously been hired to act as an usher for the evening.

"Look, Granddad, what would *you* know 'bout vampires?" the boy asked impatiently.

"How dare you!" The old man bristled. "I'll have you know I am a vampire myself!"

The boy snorted. "Yeah, right. And I'm the Queen of Sheba."

"No, you are not!" said Viktor, outraged. "I have met the Queen of Sheba. She is a very handsome lady."

"Yeah right!" The boy burst out laughing and the crowd roared as well. "She's not even real—oh wait, I bet you're goin' to tell me now that vampires are real?" He grinned.

"Well, of course they are real. I just told you—I *am* one," said Viktor in an irate tone.

The crowd laughed even harder.

"Yeah? Well, go on then. Let's see you do somethin' vampire-y," said the boy with an even bigger grin. He leaned over and tilted his head, presenting his neck. "Go on, then—bite me an' suck my blood!"

"I do not suck blood!" spluttered Viktor. "What do you think I am? A mosquito?"

"Hey, you said you're a vampire."

Viktor drew himself up to his full height. "I am indeed—but that does not mean I drink blood. Only a very small number of us vampires belong to the Order Vampyrus—most of us prefer to consume insects, fruits and nectar..." He paused, then added, "Although I did know a vampire who enjoyed small frogs, and lizards. Not unsurprising, really, since his other form was a Mexican leaf-nosed bat. Very nice gentleman, as I recall. Liked a bit of salt and a wedge of lime with his lizards."

"Uh-huh," said the boy, trying to keep a straight face. He grinned at the crowd behind Viktor's back and made a twirling motion with his finger around the side of his head, mouthing: "*Totally loopy.*"

"I, myself, am a fruitarian," added Viktor with great dignity.

"A what?"

"A fruitarian. I eat only fruits."

The boy chortled. "Yeah? You mean you suck out their juices an' make 'em undead like you?"

"Undead? I am certainly not undead! Do I look undead to you?" Viktor jutted his head out on his scrawny neck and eyeballed the teenager, who took a hasty step back.

"Okay, look, you've been a good laugh, Granddad, but you're gettin' in people's way so if you don't move along—"

"I shall not move until *you* remove this monstrosity!" declared Viktor, jabbing a finger at the poster.

"Hey, cut it out, okay?" said the boy, starting to sound really annoyed. "If you don't stop bein' a pain, I'm goin' to call the police—"

Yikes. Hastily, Caitlyn started pushing her way through the crowd towards them. "Wait! He's not—"

"Is there a problem?"

Just as Caitlyn reached Viktor, a tall, dark-haired man stepped into the circle. He didn't have to push—the crowd parted respectfully around him. He had handsome aristocratic features and a lithe muscular build, emphasised by dark jeans encasing his long legs and a crisp cotton shirt stretched across his broad shoulders. But more than his good looks, it was his air of quiet command that gave him such a strong presence.

Caitlyn's heart gave its customary jolt as she looked up into Lord James Fitzroy's keen grey eyes and she felt her pulse fluttering. She was embarrassed by her schoolgirl reaction to James every time she saw him (it was almost three months since they'd first met; surely she should have got over it by now?) but she couldn't seem to help herself. No matter how many times she saw him, meeting James again always seemed to turn her into a shy, tongue-tied, blushing mess.

"Is there a problem?" James asked again, looking at the teenage usher.

The boy rolled his eyes. "Yeah, Grandpa Fruitarian here seems to think that he's a vampire

7

and—"

"I do not 'seem to think'," said Viktor indignantly. "I *know*. I was born a vampire—and I am one of the last of my kind."

The crowd tittered again and James looked at loss for words.

"Ah, here you are! I've been looking for you everywhere," said Caitlyn with false brightness. She stepped forwards and grabbed Viktor's arm, while giving everybody a breezy smile. "Sorry! A little misunderstanding, but we're just leaving—"

"Caitlyn? Do you know this gentleman?" James asked.

"Er..." Caitlyn wondered wildly what to say. Somehow, she didn't think "*Yes, he's my vampire uncle*" would go down very well. "Um... er... sort of. This is my... uh... friend, Viktor," she mumbled.

A look of surprise, mingled with relief, crossed James's face. "*This* is Viktor?"

"Yes, why?"

"When you mentioned him before, I'd assumed that he was... er... younger," said James, clearing his throat.

It was Caitlyn's turn to look at him in surprise. She could only remember mentioning Viktor to James once before: when he had berated her for exploring the stone circle alone while a murder suspect was on the loose and she had blurted out that she had been protected by her friend, "Viktor". Instead of reassuring him, though, it had seemed to annoy James, especially when she had refused to tell him more about her mysterious male friend. In fact, Caitlyn had even fleetingly wondered if James had been jealous.

Viktor bristled at James's words. "Younger? Younger? Do you think youth is everything?" He held up two scrawny fists. "I am more than a match for you, young man! Bring out a sword and we'll have a duel! *Then* we'll see what you're really made of—"

"Uh... Viktor has a great sense of humour," Caitlyn cut in hastily with a weak smile as James stared at the old man in bewilderment. She gripped Viktor's arm. "Anyway, we've got to be going. Sorry for any misunderstanding! See you around!" she called over her shoulder as she hustled the old vampire away, leaving James, the teenage usher, and the rest of the crowd gaping after them.

Caitlyn didn't release Viktor until they were a good distance away and well out of earshot of most people.

"What are you doing here?" she demanded.

"Protecting you, of course," said Viktor huffily. "As your guardian uncle, it is my duty to watch over you and make sure that you come to no harm."

"What harm could come to me here?" asked Caitlyn, exasperated.

Viktor wagged a finger in her face. "Ah, you never know. Evil lurks in many places and—" His gaze slid over her shoulder and he drew his breath in sharply. "Aha! I found you at last!" he hissed and darted past her.

"Wha—?" Caitlyn turned to see the old vampire hovering over a row of tangled, prickly bushes. Plump red fruit were dangling in large numbers from several stems.

"Mm... wild raspberries!" Viktor smacked his lips and rubbed his hands with glee.

Caitlyn started to say something but was interrupted by the loudspeaker announcing that the film was about to begin soon. She realised that she hadn't even got the beanbags yet. Pomona would be getting worried, wondering what had happened to her! She glanced at Viktor again but the old vampire was already engrossed in plucking berries from the bushes and stuffing them into his mouth, so she shrugged and left him to it. Hopefully, the raspberries would keep him busy and out of trouble for the rest of the evening.

CHAPTER TWO

As Caitlyn joined the end of the dwindling queue in front of the beanbag booth, she wondered anxiously if they might run out by the time it came to her turn. Luckily, however, she managed to grab the last two. The beanbags were much bigger and bulkier than she had expected, however, and she decided to take the route around the edge of the lawn rather than fight her way through the crowd encamped across the centre.

The lawn was surrounded by neatly clipped hedges, interspersed with occasional flowerbeds, and as she passed one of these, she saw a group of children crouched around an enormous dog the size of a small pony. It was Bran, James Fitzroy's English mastiff. He was lying with his legs stretched out in front of him and sitting between his front paws was a little black kitten. Caitlyn broke into a smile at the sight of them.

"Hello Bran," she said softly, bending down to pat the dog.

"*Mew!*" cried the kitten indignantly.

Caitlyn laughed and patted the kitten as well. "Yes, and hello to you too, Nibs. I hope you're staying out of trouble."

"He tried to climb up my leg," said one little girl.

Caitlyn made a face. "Ouch! I hope Nibs didn't scratch you."

"He's only a baby cat so his claws aren't very sharp yet," said another little girl with a freckled face and pigtails. She scooped up the kitten and cuddled him against her. "I love you, Nibs—I wish you were mine!"

Caitlyn smiled, recognising six-year-old Molly Jenkins who lived in the village. She started to reply but, before she could say anything, they were interrupted by a volley of high-pitched barking. The children backed away and Caitlyn turned in surprise to see a small brown-and-white terrier come shooting out of the bushes nearby. It rushed up to Bran, teeth bared and hackles raised.

"*YAP-YAP-YAP-YAP-YAP!*"

The mastiff looked at the terrier in surprise. He gave a friendly thump of his tail, his wrinkled face pulled back in a placid smile, but this just seemed to provoke the terrier even more. The smaller dog snarled and lunged at Bran, nipping at his feet.

Bran jerked his paw away, looking bewildered, and gave a soft whine. He wagged his tail again, but the terrier ignored Bran's friendly overtures. Instead, it growled and launched itself at the mastiff once more.

"Hey!" cried Caitlyn, trying to step in. "Hey, hey! Leave poor Bran alone..." She bent down to try and grab the terrier by its collar but she had barely caught hold of it when a sharp voice said:

"What are you doing to my dog?"

A middle-aged woman stomped into their midst and yanked Caitlyn's hand off the terrier's collar. She was wearing a big straw hat and a baggy floral cotton dress, with green wellington boots poking out from beneath, and looked like the stereotype of the British country matron.

She glared at Caitlyn and snapped, "What were you doing to Rocco?"

"N-nothing," stammered Caitlyn. "I wasn't doing anything. I mean—he was attacking Bran so I was just trying to stop him—"

"Nonsense! Rocco would never attack anything... would you, darling?" The woman picked up the terrier in her arms. The little dog glared at Caitlyn and lifted his lip, showing a row of sharp teeth.

The woman gave Bran a dirty look. "More likely than not, it was that great big brute of a dog who tried to bully him and Rocco was just defending himself."

Caitlyn started to protest, then she glanced at

Bran. The mastiff was unharmed and didn't seem that bothered by what had happened. With an inward sigh, she decided it would be easier to let things go. She'd met dog owners like this before and they were always convinced that their little darlings could do no wrong, no matter what evidence to the contrary. So she bit her lip and said nothing as the woman gave Bran another dirty look, then turned and stalked off with the terrier still in her arms.

"It's not true, what she said," piped up a small voice next to Caitlyn. "That mean doggie *did* attack Bran!"

Caitlyn glanced down to see Molly's indignant little face. She dropped to her knees next to the girl. "I know, sweetie, but sometimes... well, sometimes people see what they want to see and it's hard to change their minds." She reached out to pat Bran's big head again. "Anyway, the important thing is— Bran's all right, isn't he?"

The child placed the kitten back on the ground and looked at the mastiff, who was panting amiably. "Bran's hot," she said.

"Yes, it's quite warm, isn't it?" agreed Caitlyn.

Molly extended her right hand and uncurled her pudgy fingers to show a sticky brown blob in her palm. "Look. My chocolate's melted," she said forlornly.

"Aww... I'm sorry," said Caitlyn, reaching out to touch the piece gently with her forefinger. There was a tingle in her fingertip and the brown blob shimmered, then rippled out into a smooth, glossy bar of milk chocolate.

"Oh!" cried Molly in delight, staring down at the chocolate bar in her hand. "You did magic!"

Caitlyn drew her hand back hastily. She wasn't sure what had happened. This was one aspect of her new-found witch powers which still frightened her sometimes: the way she couldn't control the magic inside her.

"How did you make it do that?" asked Molly, as the other children gathered around her and stared at the perfectly smooth chocolate bar.

"I... I don't know... I mean, I didn't do anything," said Caitlyn. She glanced furtively at the other children, wondering if they would recoil in fear. She knew that there was a lot of prejudice in the village against witchcraft, and the children must have heard negative comments from their parents. But to her relief, they were all Molly's age and still young enough to happily believe in magic. In fact, instead of fear, there was wistful envy on their faces as they looked at the chocolate in Molly's hand.

"Can I have one too?" asked another little girl, extending her palm towards Caitlyn.

Caitlyn hesitated. She really shouldn't have been practising magic in public, but with the little girl looking at her so hopefully, she didn't have the heart to say no. Before she realised what she was doing, she had stretched out a finger and touched the little girl's palm. A second later, a perfectly formed chocolate bar appeared.

"Ooh! Thank you!" squealed the little girl.

A little boy thrust his hand towards her. "Me too, miss! I want a chocolate bar too!"

"And me!"

"Yes, me too, please!"

In a flash, Caitlyn was surrounded by eager little faces and a circle of open palms. Swallowing her misgivings, she glanced around to make sure no adults were watching, then quickly tapped each hand in turn. As the last child thanked her and turned away, happily clutching a piece of chocolate, Caitlyn hoped that they wouldn't tell their parents how they'd got the sweets. *Maybe the adults would put it down to the children's vivid imagination, anyway*, Caitlyn thought. If she was accused of anything, she could always say that she had produced the chocolates from her pocket, using a sleight-of-hand magic trick.

Feeling a little bit better, she grabbed the beanbags again and turned to go. But she had forgotten about the kitten who was now demanding some attention.

"*Mew!*" cried Nibs, clambering up on one of the beanbags.

Caitlyn gave the kitten a hurried pat, then lifted him off the beanbag and set him on the ground. "Sorry, Nibs—I haven't got time to play with you now. I've got to get these beanbags back to Pomona."

But the kitten wasn't taking no for an answer. He darted between her legs as she began walking again, causing her to trip and stumble. Caitlyn gasped and fell, collapsing onto Bran, who was still lying on the grass next to them.

"Oomph!"

Luckily, the mastiff's furry bulk had cushioned her fall. He turned his head and looked at her quizzically, as she lay flopped across his back, then gave the side of her face a hearty lick.

"Eeuuw!" Caitlyn recoiled from his huge wet tongue.

She started trying to roll off his back but Bran decided at the same moment to heave himself to his feet. Caitlyn flailed around as the mastiff's huge body lurched up. His rump swung against her, knocking her over once more, and she pitched forwards, face down in the grass, bum in the air.

"Are you all right?" a male voice asked and she felt a gentle hand on her elbow.

For a moment, she thought that it was James Fitzroy and she was mortified, imagining how she must look. But as she rose, flushing, she realised that it was another man. He was just as tall and just as handsome as James—but in a very different way. His dark eyes were midnight blue, fringed by ridiculously long lashes, and his black hair was slicked back to leave a slight widow's peak on his forehead. He had a full, sensual mouth and a shadow of stubble across his chiselled jawline, giving him the sexy look of a man who had just got out of bed. His muscled torso was outlined by the navy T-shirt he wore and she could see dark chest hairs curling over edges of the V neckline.

"*Mademoiselle*, are you all right?" he asked again, and this time Caitlyn realised that he spoke with a French accent.

"Er... yes, thank you," said Caitlyn, brushing her hair out of her face. She was trying hard not to stare. She had never met a man quite so... well, so *beautiful*.

"These bags of bean are too cumbersome for one so dainty as you, *n'est-ce pas*?" He tilted his head, smiling at her.

Dainty? Caitlyn had never thought of her pear-shaped figure as dainty. She had always been self-conscious about her wide hips and thighs—and yet this man was looking at her in a way that made her feel like the slim, petite women she had always envied.

She returned his smile. "They... they *are* a bit bulky. But I suppose they need to be, to provide the support, otherwise they'd sag, you know, in the middle when you sit down. But maybe that depends on how heavy you are too—not that I know, really, as I haven't tried them..." She realised that she was blabbing like an idiot and trailed off awkwardly.

The stranger's eyes twinkled. "*Moi aussi*. This is not the first time I have encountered such bags of bean for seating but it shall certainly be my first experience watching a film on them. My tastes tend to be more traditional; in my *chateau* in France, the chairs for the outdoors are in wrought iron—or perhaps solid wood—but *alors*, my friend, James, he is a great one for new ideas and new ways of doing things."

"James? I mean, Lord Fitzroy? You're his friend?"

The stranger made a slight bow which would have looked silly and theatrical on any other man. "*Mais oui.* Allow me to introduce myself: my name is Antoine de Villiers." He raised a teasing eyebrow, a smile curling the corners of his mouth. "And may I be so bold as to ask for *mademoiselle's* name in return?"

"It's... it's Caitlyn," she said, giving him another smile. "Caitlyn Le Fey."

He took her hand, raising it to his lips. "Caitlyn." He said the name slowly, like someone savouring a fine wine. "A beautiful name. For a beautiful woman."

Caitlyn realised suddenly that he was flirting with her. She felt herself blushing as his lips pressed the back of her hand. Hastily, she drew it away.

Clearing her throat, she asked, "Um... are you visiting James?"

He inclined his head. "I have not seen him since our days at Oxford together. *Alors*, I decided a visit was long overdue." His eyes lingered over her again and he gave her a suggestive smile. "Of course, had

I known what pleasures lay in wait here in Tillyhenge, I might have come much sooner."

Caitlyn blushed again. His flirting was outrageous—and yet she couldn't help feeling flattered. No one had ever looked at her in this way. Even when James Fitzroy paid her a compliment, he was so restrained and polite—whereas there was something thrilling about this Frenchman's bold admiration.

The sound of the voice from the loudspeaker brought her out of her thoughts.

"Oh! I've got to go. My cousin is waiting for me…"

"You will permit me to assist you?" Antoine gestured to the beanbags.

"Oh… thanks. That's really kind of you." Caitlyn surrendered the unwieldy lumps gratefully.

CHAPTER THREE

When they returned to Pomona's spot on the lawn, they found her engrossed in conversation with an elderly gentleman.

"Caitlyn! Where have you been? I was just gonna come and look for y—" Pomona broke off as she caught sight of Antoine de Villiers. Her eyebrows climbed so high that they almost disappeared into her hairline.

"Er... this is my cousin, Pomona Sinclair," said Caitlyn. "And this is Antoine—Antoine de Villiers. He's a friend of James."

"*Enchanté, mademoiselle,*" said Antoine, clasping Pomona's hand and raising it to his lips. His eyes flickered to the elderly gentleman.

Pomona took the hint and gestured towards the other man. "This is Mr Rochat," she said, giving it the French pronunciation of "*Ro-shah*".

Antoine paused slightly, then extended his hand. The old man grasped it briefly. Caitlyn was surprised at their offhand reactions—she would have thought that two Frenchmen meeting each other would respond more warmly. But then, maybe that was a silly thought. After all, two Americans meeting each other in a foreign country wouldn't be instant best friends just because they were both Americans. In any case, she had a feeling that a man like Antoine de Villiers wasted no charm on other males—his attention was focused solely on the ladies.

"*Alors*, I must go," he said, turning back to Caitlyn with a smile. "James will be looking for me. But I hope we will meet again soon. *À bientôt*, mademoiselle." He made a slight bow, then turned and strode away.

"Jeez, you've been gone forever," complained Pomona.

"Sorry, I got a bit sidetracked," said Caitlyn.

Pomona rolled her eyes. "Yeah, I can see that..."

"Oh, no... I didn't mean Antoine..." Caitlyn stammered. "There was some trouble with Bran and another dog... and the children... Anyway..." She smiled at the gentleman next to them. "You looked like you were having a good time with Mr Rochat."

"Please, call me Pierre," said the old man.

Caitlyn looked at him curiously. His English was fluent and, unlike Antoine de Villiers, he hardly had a hint of a French accent. He was dressed very formally for a casual outdoor event, in an old-fashioned tweed jacket, waistcoat, and pressed trousers, with a scarlet silk kerchief tucked jauntily into the lapel pocket.

His eyes were shrewd behind his spectacles as he smiled at Caitlyn and said, "Your cousin has been telling me much about you and the interesting experiences you have been having in the last few months."

Caitlyn glanced at Pomona, wondering what she had told him. Pomona had the typical American confidence and ease in conversing with total strangers—something that Caitlyn usually envied—but sometimes Pomona's bubbly personality also meant that she shared far more than she should have about her private life. Caitlyn hoped her cousin hadn't divulged too much.

"I understand that you recently discovered that you were adopted?" Pierre Rochat asked. "Your mother was Barbara Le Fey, the celebrated singer?"

Caitlyn nodded cautiously. "Yes, she was my adoptive mother. She died a few months ago in a car crash and I learned after the funeral that she adopted me as a baby."

"And your real family? They are here in England?"

"Yeah, they're right here in Tillyhenge!" beamed Pomona. "Can you believe the coincidence? Caitlyn wandered into the village chocolate shop as soon as she arrived and guess what? Turns out that the owner is her grandmother! And she's also got an aunt and cousin who—"

"Yes, well, I'm sure Mr Rochat doesn't want to be bored by my family history," cut in Caitlyn. She gave the man a bright smile. "So, are you just visiting Tillyhenge or do you live in the area?"

"Please, call me Pierre," he said again with old-fashioned courtesy. "I am a dealer in antique jewellery. I happened to be visiting a colleague in Gloucester and heard about the new Open-Air Cinema being held in the grounds of Huntingdon Manor. It sounded like a delightful way to spend an evening and the film sounded most interesting, so... here I am." He smiled at her.

"Oh, right," said Caitlyn. She wouldn't have expected someone like Pierre Rochat to be into vampire movies. He seemed more the type to enjoy art-house films or war biopics. But maybe appearances were deceptive. After all, there were probably tattooed bikers who enjoyed romantic comedies and white-haired old grannies who liked horror movies.

The giant screen in front of them flickered suddenly to life. Caitlyn glanced across the lawn and realised that twilight had fallen while they were talking. The sky was now a deep indigo blue and silhouetted against it, looming up behind them, was Huntingdon Manor. The windows were all lit— shimmering squares of gold arranged in perfect symmetry—and it looked beautiful and slightly unreal, like an English country manor in a historical romance novel.

A hush fell over the crowd as music began blaring from the speakers and a series of advertisements played across the screen. Pomona leaned across and said to Pierre Rochat:

"Hey, do you wanna share a beanbag? I feel kinda bad that you're sitting on the ground—"

"No, no… do not worry on my account. In fact, I think I will go and get a drink. I believe I saw a booth selling refreshments." He rose to his feet.

Pomona looked at him in surprise. "But the movie's starting," she protested.

The old man didn't appear to hear her. He gave them a perfunctory wave and hurried away, his figure soon swallowed by the darkness. Pomona watched him go for a moment, then shrugged and leaned back to watch the movie. Caitlyn settled down in her own beanbag as the opening credits rolled across the screen. The camera panned over a dark forest landscape, zooming in at last on a Gothic castle perched on the edge of the cliff. A flock of bats swerved past the castle spires and mist swirled around the turrets.

Caitlyn rolled her eyes at the clichés and rolled them even more when the scene cut to the interior of the castle. In a large hall with a gaudy chandelier, a man lay sleeping in an open coffin. He was very pale, with black hair smoothed back from a high forehead, and a haughty expression, which would have made him look frightening—except that he was snoring loudly. The audience laughed. Then a full moon came into view in the open window and the man woke up. He rose gracefully from the coffin—and smacked his head on the low-hanging chandelier.

"OWWW!" He hopped around in fury, rubbing his head.

The crowd roared with laughter again and Caitlyn gave a wry smile. This looked like it was going to be a very silly movie. Still, it was a lovely summer evening and it was nice to be spending time with Pomona. She relaxed against the beanbag, chuckling as the vampire stalked down the staircase of his castle, his black cape billowing dramatically behind him—only to catch on a rusty nail, making him trip and nearly fall down the stairs. Regaining his balance and his dignity, he morphed into a bat and flew to the nearby village, straight into the bedroom window of an unlucky maiden. In a flash, he was perched on the edge of her bed, ready to sink his teeth into her lily-white neck. There was an appreciative gasp from the audience as he opened his mouth, revealing long white fangs, and then the heroine opened her eyes and screamed shrilly.

A second later, there was another scream. A bloodcurdling scream of fear and horror. For a moment, Caitlyn thought it had come from the movie as well, then she noticed various people next to her sitting up and looking around. A murmur of anxiety passed through crowd. Caitlyn realised suddenly that the second scream had been real.

"What's going on?" asked Pomona.

"I don't know," murmured Caitlyn.

She stood up and craned her neck. She could see a crowd forming at the opposite edge of the lawn. Curious, she hurried across and pushed her way through the circle of people gathered around something on the ground. Then she stopped short as she saw what they were staring at. It was the body of a man. A farmer crouched down and felt for a pulse, then shook his head. Several torches played over the body, which was twisted awkwardly so that the head was tilted back and the neck was showing. There was a gasp from the crowd as a beam of light fell on the side of his throat. Two deep puncture wounds were clearly visible—puncture wounds that looked like fang marks.

"It's a vampire! He's been killed by a vampire!" somebody screamed.

"Yes, look! See the bite on his neck!"

"Oh my God..."

"No!"

"But... it can't be... Vampires aren't real!"

Caitlyn stared at the body, barely hearing the hysterical cries around her. She had just recognised the man lying there. It was Pierre Rochat. She felt a sense of disbelief. She had only been talking to him a few minutes ago! He had been sitting next to her, alive and healthy. Now his skin was deathly pale, his eyes empty and staring.

Then there came another cry: "Over there! In the bushes! Who's that?"

The beams of light swung wildly, raking over the bushes behind the body. There was a furtive movement, and, the next minute, a familiar figure was caught in the harsh glare. Caitlyn stiffened at the sight: it was Viktor. He was standing, hunched over, with his mouth smeared red and two long fangs protruding from his lips.

"It's him!" somebody shrieked. "It's the vampire!"

"SEIZE HIM!"

The crowd surged forwards. Caitlyn tried to protest but her voice was lost as she was jostled and pushed aside. She found herself shoved to the back of the circle as people began to shout and yell.

"We need to call the police!"

"No time for that—we have to seize him first!"

"Yes! A citizen's arrest!"

"What if he attacks you?"

"Has anyone got garlic?"

"No, but I have some garlic bread—will that do?"

Two burly farmers grabbed Viktor by the shoulders and hauled the old man forwards to face the crowd.

The elderly vampire spluttered, trying to free himself. "What is the meaning of this? Unhand me at once, sir!"

"Not 'til the police get here, you murderer," growled one of the farmers.

"Murderer? I have not murdered anyone."

"You liar!" cried a woman, pointing at his mouth. "There's blood on them fangs! You killed 'im and drank 'is blood!"

"Nonsense!" Viktor snapped. "I do not drink blood. I am a fruitarian. I have been feasting on some wild raspberries and—"

"Tie him up!"

"Gag him!"

"He's a vampire—you've got to drive a stake through his heart—"

"NO!" Caitlyn gasped.

She couldn't believe what she was hearing. This was the twenty-first century; surely people didn't still believe in superstitions like that? But she knew that crowd mania could be a dangerous thing: people got hysterical and caught up in the emotion of the moment. She had read enough newspaper reports of terrible deaths when a mob got out of control—and that was before you added in the fear of the paranormal.

Caitlyn shoved herself against the circle, trying to squeeze between people and get to the front. "Stop! He's not a murderer! Please... he's just an old man—"

"*Police!* Let us through, please."

Caitlyn sagged with relief as she saw the tall figure of James Fitzroy moving through the crowd, accompanied by several uniformed constables and a grizzled CID detective with a neat moustache and world-weary air: Detective Inspector Walsh. The crowd parted respectfully as the police approached the body.

Inspector Walsh's face was grim as he looked down at the victim. "Who discovered the body?" he asked.

There was a murmur of confusion through the crowd.

"Dunno... it was here when I arrived..."

"...thought you found it—"

"No, I thought *you* did..."

"There was a scream. Did you hear it?"

"...and I told my missus, we ought to go and see what the fuss is about..."

"PLEASE!" Inspector Walsh held both hands up. "Can the person who found the body step forward?"

There was an expectant hush. Everyone looked around but nobody stepped out of the crowd.

"*Some*body must have discovered the body," said Inspector Walsh. "Otherwise, how did you all know to come over?"

"There was a scream," a women piped up, and everyone around her nodded.

The inspector sighed. "Yes, and it stands to reason that the person who screamed was the one who found the body. So who screamed?"

Again, there was no movement from the crowd, other than people looking curiously around. Caitlyn shared the inspector's growing exasperation. Had the person who'd found the body run away? Why weren't they owning up?

Inspector Walsh looked around the circle. "All right, then... This scream—was it by a man or a woman?"

"A man!"

"No, a woman!"

"Definitely a woman."

"I thought it was a man."

Before Walsh could say anything else, the two burly farmers stepped forwards, thrusting Viktor in front of them.

"Here, sir. We've apprehended him for you."

"That's right. Caught 'im red-handed, we did."

The inspector looked nonplussed. "I'm sorry... and this gentleman is?"

"The murderer!" said a woman, pointing at Viktor. "He's the vampire!"

"The *what*?"

"Yes, sir—him's the one who's done it, sir," another man spoke up. "Him's the killer."

"I did not kill anyone!" Viktor started spluttering again but he was cut off by several voices.

"He's lyin', sir!" a woman yelled. "He did it!"

Her friend nodded vehemently. "Attacked that poor chap and sucked the blood right out o' him!"

A man pointed at the body. "See them marks on his neck? Those are fang marks, sir!"

"What nonsense is this?" asked Inspector Walsh

irritably.

"It's not nonsense, sir! This man's a vampire."

"Yeah, he said so himself!" cried a new voice.

Caitlyn turned to see a young man pushing his way to the front of the crowd. Her heart sank as she recognised the teenage usher from earlier. He was practically dancing with excitement as he jabbed a finger at Viktor. "I know him! He was givin' me grief earlier, insistin' that I take down the poster for the movie... an' he said he was a vampire."

Several people gasped. "So he confessed?"

"Confess? Why would I confess?" asked Viktor. "I am not ashamed of what I am! I belong to a noble order—"

"You see! He's admittin' it!"

"Did you hear that? Proud of being a killer, he is!"

"PLEASE!" The inspector put his hands up again. "I must ask you all to move back—this is a crime scene now. If you could stand back and wait for one of the constables to come and take your statement, I'd be much obliged." He glanced at the two farmers. "And you may release this gentleman. I will take responsibility for him now."

Reluctantly, the crowd began following his instructions. Caitlyn, however, ignored the police officers. Instead, she pushed her way through until she reached Inspector Walsh's side. He was now questioning Viktor, with James watching silently.

"...may I ask where you were when you heard the

scream?"

"I was in the woods, there—" Viktor pointed at the bushes behind them. "I was hurrying through the trees, thinking someone may need my assistance, and unfortunately collided with one in my haste, then—"

"Was anyone with you?"

"No, but—"

"So no one can vouch for your whereabouts at the time of the murder?"

Viktor bridled with offended dignity. "Are you implying that I am lying?"

"I am suggesting, sir, that we only have your word that you were moving *towards* the body when the others saw you. For all we know, you could have actually been running *away* from the body." Inspector Walsh paused significantly. "In other words, fleeing the scene of the crime after committing the murder." His eyes flickered over Viktor's appearance, taking in the red-stained mouth. "I'm afraid, Mr... er...?"

"Dracul. Count Viktor Dracul is my proper name." Viktor swept him a bow.

Inspector Walsh looked slightly taken aback. "Er... right. Mr... er... Dracul... well, given the circumstances, I'm afraid I will have to take you in for questioning. If you will be kind enough to accompany me down to the police station—"

"You're not arresting him?" gasped Caitlyn. "No, no... there's been a misunderstanding." She looked frantically at James. "You met Viktor earlier—you know he's not a murderer."

"Caitlyn..." James looked uncomfortable. "I don't really know this gentleman at all."

The inspector frowned at her. "I am not arresting anyone... yet. However, as Lord Fitzroy knows, the police have the right to detain any suspect in a murder investigation. Mr Dracul himself has no objection to being questioned. Now, Miss Le Fey, I'd appreciate if you'd stand back and let the police do their job."

He turned to go, then paused to have a brief word with James. Caitlyn took the opportunity to grab Viktor's arm and pull him slightly aside.

"Viktor—you can change!" she whispered in his ear. "Shift into your bat form. Then you can escape."

"I am not running away like a coward. I have committed no crime and I am not afraid to face questioning. It is the right and honourable thing to do to remain and assist the police in their investigation. I am sure once they have heard my side of the story, they will see that I am innocent and—"

Caitlyn groaned. "Viktor, you don't understand! It doesn't always work like that. Innocent people get arrested and charged for crimes they didn't commit, especially when all the circumstantial evidence points towards them and there's no other suspect. Look, it'll be much simpler if you just...

disappeared."

"No." He shook his head firmly. "It is a matter of honour. I will not slink away like a guilty criminal when I have done nothing to be ashamed of."

Before she could say anything else, he lifted his chin and walked away from her to join the inspector. Caitlyn could only stand and watch helplessly as the old vampire was led away by the police.

CHAPTER FOUR

The movie was cancelled, of course, although most of the crowd lingered, hoping to catch a glimpse of the "vampire murderer" or pick up some gossip. The forensics team arrived, as well as an ambulance to remove the body, and Caitlyn found herself being shepherded, along with the people who had found Rochat, into the Library at the Manor to await questioning. James had organised for hot drinks and food to be brought, and there was plenty of comfortable seating—not to mention shelves of books to browse. Soon the group became quite jolly, speculating and exchanging wild theories about the "vampire murderer". But Caitlyn sat to one side, trying not to listen and wishing she could get the questioning over with.

It was a long night. By the time she had given

her statement to a harassed-looking constable, it was nearly midnight. Caitlyn walked wearily out of the Library to find Pomona and James standing outside. Her heart skipped a beat at the thought that James might have been waiting especially to make sure that she was all right.

"Omigod, Caitlyn—I thought you were never gonna get out!" said Pomona.

"You look tired," said James gently. "I was just suggesting to Pomona that perhaps you'd like to stay the night?"

"And I've accepted!" added Pomona, before Caitlyn could answer.

Caitlyn gave James a wan smile. "Thanks, but I'm sure things are chaotic enough with the murder. I don't want to give you any more trouble—"

"Not at all. I'd been meaning to invite you and Pomona to come and stay at the Manor for a few days, anyway. I have a group of friends arriving from London the day after tomorrow and would be delighted if you could join us. It would be a small country house party of sorts—"

"That sounds awesome!" Pomona said before Caitlyn could reply again.

"What about the Widow Mags?" asked Caitlyn. "We've been helping her in the chocolate shop—"

"Oh, she can spare us for a few days," said Pomona, waving a hand.

"I've already sent a message to let her know that you won't be returning tonight," said James. "And

I'm sure Pomona is right. The Widow Mags won't mind you staying at the Manor for a few days. You can always pop back to the village during the day if you're needed."

Caitlyn gave in, and a few minutes later they were shown to a large suite with twin beds and sumptuous cream and gold furnishings. Pomona flopped onto one of the beds as soon as the door shut behind them and bounced up and down like a little girl.

"Omigod, this is awesome! Just like when we were kids and had those sleepovers together! Well, except this is a lot more impressive than your mom's trailer or even our house in Beverley Hills," she said, looking around at the period furniture and elegant upholstery. "We used to stay up all night and talk—and then when your Nanny came to check on us, we'd hide under the covers— remember?"

Caitlyn smiled, feeling her mood lighten. Yes, she did remember. As the daughter of a world-famous singer with itchy feet, Caitlyn had practically grown up on the road. Even when they hadn't been on tour or visiting music festivals, her adoptive mother, Barbara Le Fey, had preferred to live in various "holiday homes" around the world, rather than her house in L.A. She felt that she wrote her best music when she was always on the move. It might have seemed like a glamorous lifestyle, but it had also been a lonely one for Caitlyn, who had never got the chance to put down roots or make any real friends. Barbara herself had been a kind but distant mother, too wrapped up in her career to pay more than cursory attention to the little girl she had adopted on a whim.

But the one constant in Caitlyn's life had been her cousin, Pomona—Barbara's sister's daughter. With her big blonde hair, long tanned limbs, and bubbly personality, Pomona was everything that the shy, bookish Caitlyn was not... and yet the two girls had quickly become best friends. Those times when Pomona came to visit had been the highlights of her childhood. Now Caitlyn flashed back to the nights she and Pomona had spent giggling together in the darkness, and the enthusiastic pillow fights they used to have.

As if reading her thoughts, Pomona suddenly grabbed one of the pillows and squealed with delight as she squeezed it. "Man! These are serious feather pillows!" She laughed. "Remember how I used to beat you at all the pillow fights?"

"You did not! I remember you running away, squealing like a pig—"

"No way! You were the one who used to squeal—"

"I never squealed!

"Oh yeah? We'll see about that!"

Pomona tossed the pillow across the room. Caitlyn barely had time to catch it before her cousin had sprung off the bed with another pillow and rushed towards her, waving it over her head.

"Yeeeeaaahh!"

"Wait! Stop, Pomie—we can't! We shouldn't—we're going to mess up the room—"

Caitlyn said, trying not to laugh as she ducked from her cousin.

"Aww, c'mon! Where's your sense of fun?" cried Pomona and smacked the pillow against Caitlyn's head.

Caitlyn staggered back, and then, before she realised what she was doing, she'd retaliated by flinging her own pillow at Pomona.

"Whoopee!" Pomona yelled, ducking away.

Caitlyn chased after her, forgetting all about her own protests. A feeling of carefree recklessness filled her. They ran around the room, laughing and pummelling each other with their pillows, and Caitlyn couldn't remember the last time she'd had so much fun.

"Na-na-na-na-na... you can't get me!" sang Pomona, pausing in front of the bedroom door and taunting Caitlyn with rude faces.

"Oh yeah? Watch this!" Caitlyn rushed towards her cousin, swinging her pillow in a wide arc overhead.

Pomona darted sideways at the last minute, just as the door swung open. Caitlyn gasped but it was too late—she couldn't stop the pillow as it smacked James Fitzroy straight in the face.

Whumph!

He reeled backwards as the pillow bounced off

his head, and feathers drifted everywhere.

"Oh!" Caitlyn froze, horrified. Behind her, she could hear peals of laughter from Pomona. "I... I... I'm so sorry..."

She squirmed. Why couldn't she ever meet James in a graceful, sophisticated manner?

James blinked a few times. Then he cleared his throat and said, "I was heading to my own room and heard some cries... I just wanted to make sure you were all right."

Caitlyn flushed, wondering what he was thinking as he looked at the state of the room. "Um... yes, we're fine. Sorry, we got a bit carried away—"

James broke into a smile, his grey eyes twinkling. "I used to have pillow fights with my sister when we were children," he said with a chuckle. "She was only half my size but she still used to wallop me!"

Caitlyn returned his smile, grateful for his understanding. Then she sobered. "Have... have you heard anything more from the police?" she asked. "What's happening to Viktor?"

"They're keeping him in custody overnight. I believe Inspector Walsh wants to question him again tomorrow, after he has spoken to some other witnesses."

"You can't let them charge Viktor for murder," Caitlyn pleaded. "He had nothing to do with it. He's just a harmless old man."

"Inspector Walsh is a good detective," said James

gently. "I'm sure he will consider all the evidence carefully without jumping to any conclusions. In the meantime, do you know if Viktor has any family or friends who need to be notified? I assume he will be contacting his solicitor from the police station."

"Um... I... er... I'm not sure. I don't really know that much about his private life."

James said nothing, but it was obvious from his look that he thought it very odd she should be concerned about an old man she seemed to know so little about. Pomona clearly thought the same. When James bid them goodnight and left, she turned to Caitlyn and demanded:

"Why are you so worried about this Viktor guy? I mean, he's just, like, some random old dude who came to the Open-Air Cinema... Why do you care if he gets arrested?"

Caitlyn hesitated. "He's not just some 'random old dude'... He's... um... a friend."

"A friend?" Pomona looked at her in disbelief. "Since when did you make friends with a nutty old geriatric?"

"Well, actually, Viktor is more like... er... family, really..."

"*Family?*"

"Yes, he's... well... Viktor is my uncle. My vampire uncle."

"Your *what?*" Pomona's mouth fell open.

"Look, it's a bit hard to explain... I met him when I first arrived in England—in fact, the day I was driving out to Tillyhenge. He was waiting by my rented car and he told me that he was my vampire uncle."

"And you believed him? I mean, how do you know he didn't escape from a nursing home or something—"

"No, Pomie, he's the real deal. He's a vampire."

Pomona put her hands up. "Wait, wait, wait... you're telling me he *is* the murderer?"

"No! No, of course not! He would never attack anyone."

"Does he have fangs?"

"Yes." *When he hasn't lost them somewhere,* Caitlyn thought.

"Well, that guy who got murdered had fang marks in his neck, right?"

"Yes, but not all vampires drink blood—Viktor's a fruitarian, actually. He only eats fruit. Because he shifts into a fruit bat, you see."

"Huh? No way! That old man is a shape-shifter?" asked Pomona, her face a mixture of incredulity and horror.

"Yes. Viktor changes into a bat, although he says he can change into other things too."

"No, no, you've gotta be wrong! Shape-shifters are, like, hot guys with killer abs who turn into alpha wolves—"

Caitlyn laughed in spite of herself. Pomona's dismay was so comical. "I guess the romance novels got things wrong. Or maybe there are some hunky young shape-shifters out there... but Viktor's not one of them. He's quite cute, though, in his bat form—he's sort of a fuzzy brown fruit bat with big black eyes. A bit like a cuddly toy. A rather grumpy cuddly toy."

Pomona looked like she was still trying to wrap her head around the idea of a stooped, balding old man being a shape-shifter.

"So he's your *uncle*?"

"Well, not a real uncle. More like a guardian uncle, I guess. He keeps talking about needing to watch over and protect me—and I have to admit, Viktor got me out of a few tight spots. In fact, he was the one who brought me the protective herb bouquet when I had to deal with that bonfire on Midsummer's Eve. If Viktor hadn't been there, I don't know what I would have done."

"If he's been around all this time, how come I never knew about him?" Pomona asked, frowning.

Caitlyn gave her an apologetic look. "Sorry, Pomie—I suppose I should have told you earlier. It's just that you guys never happened to meet and... anyway, Viktor sort of does his own thing a lot of the time." She gave a dry laugh. "Actually, he seems to spend a lot of his time looking for his teeth—he's always losing his fangs." She sighed. "I just hope he's okay at the police station. He might be a vampire but he's also a very old man."

Pomona's face softened. "I'm sure he'll be fine. You can check on him first thing in the morning."

Caitlyn nodded. She bent down to pick up the dropped pillow. "Come on—we'd better get to sleep."

CHAPTER FIVE

Caitlyn had a restless night. She kept seeing Pierre Rochat's body in her dreams, with his wide staring eyes and alabaster skin, and the fang marks in his neck... and somewhere behind his body lurked a shadowy figure... a vampire? But who was it?

When she finally opened her eyes and sat up blearily, she realised from the light streaming in through the curtains that it was already mid-morning.

"Pomie! Get up!" She went over to the other bed and gave her cousin a prod. "We've overslept!"

The other girl just burrowed her face deeper into the pillows and mumbled something unintelligible. Caitlyn sighed as she remembered how difficult it was to rouse Pomona in the mornings. Giving up, she took herself to the bathroom to shower and dress. As she brushed her hair, she wandered over to look out the bedroom windows. This side of the Manor faced the lawn which had been used for the outdoor cinema last night. In fact, the giant screen was still standing at the far end. And below her, near the site where the body had been discovered, were James and Inspector Walsh, together with a few other police officers.

Caitlyn threw her towel down and rushed out of the bedroom, running down the main staircase and out to the lawn as fast as she could. Panting, she arrived just in time to hear Inspector Walsh say:

"...speaking to the antique dealer, Mr Digweed, in Gloucester. He came forward this morning to say that he was a colleague of Pierre Rochat and had seen the man the day before. He remembers Rochat being very interested at the mention of the Tillyhenge Open-Air Cinema and expressing great enthusiasm for the idea... although that could simply have been an act. Rochat may have known about the cinema event all along but pretended he didn't, just so he could use it as an excuse to come to the village."

"You mean, he had been planning to come to Tillyhenge for another reason and the cinema was a cover?" Caitlyn spoke up. "I thought it was strange that he would come to watch a vampire movie."

The two men turned to look at her.

James smiled warmly. "Good morning. Did you sleep well?"

"Yes, thanks," said Caitlyn, giving him a shy smile in return. "Sorry, we overslept... actually, Pomona's still in bed."

James chuckled. "I get the feeling that your cousin is more of an owl than a lark."

Caitlyn rolled her eyes. "You have no idea. Trying to get her out of bed in the mornings is like trying to dig something up from underground."

Inspector Walsh cleared his throat. "You felt that Pierre Rochat's behaviour yesterday was suspicious, Miss Le Fey?" he asked.

"Well, I don't know if you'd call it suspicious. Just a bit... odd, I guess. I remember thinking that he didn't seem like the sort of man who'd be into vampire movies—although I suppose appearances can be deceptive. And the other thing that was weird was that he didn't bring anything to sit on."

"I beg your pardon?"

"For the movie," Caitlyn explained. "Everyone had come with cushions and blankets and things... but he didn't have anything. I remember thinking that was strange. Like—if you'd come to spend two hours watching a movie, you'd bring something to be comfortable on, wouldn't you? But he was just sitting on the grass. Pomona even offered to share her beanbag with him, but he declined. Then he got up just as the movie was starting and said something about getting a drink—and walked off."

"Hmm... yes, you mentioned that in your statement," said Inspector Walsh, stroking his moustache. "That does sound as if he had no intention of watching the film."

"It sounds like he was waiting for the cover of darkness and the distraction of the film to prevent anyone from noticing his activities," commented James. "The question is, what *was* he doing in Tillyhenge if he hadn't come for the Open-Air Cinema?"

"What about Viktor?" asked Caitlyn tentatively.

Inspector Walsh's face was inscrutable. "Mr Dracul is still helping us with the investigation. He is remaining at the station at present."

"You don't seriously believe that he could murder anyone? He's just a harmless old man!"

"I regret to say, Miss Le Fey, that I have known many old people who were dangerous individuals. Criminal tendencies don't disappear simply because you age." He looked at her evenly. "In any case, there is Mr Dracul's own testimony to consider, and the fact that he was found lurking near the body, with a red-stained mouth... especially in light of the... er... wounds on the victim's neck."

Caitlyn looked at him disbelievingly. "I thought you didn't believe in the paranormal. Are you saying you think a vampire killed Pierre Rochat?"

"No, of course not," growled the inspector. "All that talk of vampires is a lot of nonsense. In fact, the forensic pathologist is performing the autopsy this morning and I am sure she will find an alternative—non-supernatural—explanation for the puncture marks on the victim's neck. However, I am aware that there are people who may try to hide their crimes under the guise of a supernatural attack."

"What do you mean?" asked Caitlyn, frowning.

"He means that someone may be trying to cover up their crime by making it look like a 'vampire murder'," said James. "There have been some real-life cases of serial killers who have pretended to be—or believed they were—vampires, and they drank the blood of their victims."

"Eeuugghh..." Caitlyn recoiled from the image. She turned to Inspector Walsh. "But surely you don't think Viktor is a serial killer? He was simply in the wrong place at the wrong time!"

The detective regarded her curiously. "You seem to take a keen interest in Mr Dracul's welfare. Do you have a relationship with the gentleman?"

"Er... I..." Caitlyn licked her lips. "He's a good friend."

The inspector raised his eyebrows. "Have you known him for long?"

"No.... um... I met him when I arrived in England, actually."

"And when was that?"

"Um... back in May."

"So you have only been acquainted with him for less than three months?"

There was nothing accusatory in his tone and yet Caitlyn felt defensive.

"Yes," she said. "I know that doesn't seem like long but sometimes you just hit it off with someone as soon as you meet them, right? And I'm telling you—I know Viktor. He's not a murderer. He's just... he's just a sweet old man." She squirmed slightly. *Okay, "sweet old man" might be taking it a bit far.* "Plus... that wasn't blood on his lips. That was raspberry juice—"

"Yes, I know," Inspector Walsh admitted. "Forensics have examined Mr Dracul and concluded that there is nothing suspicious on his person, including no trace of the victim... and vice versa."

"So that means you can't hold him, right?" asked Caitlyn quickly. "You can only hold someone for twenty-four hours before you have to charge them. And you have to have proper evidence to charge someone."

Inspector Walsh hesitated, then sighed and said, "Actually, we are entitled to hold a suspect in custody for up to ninety-six hours in the case of a serious crime such as murder—however, in this case, if no further evidence comes to light linking Mr Dracul to the victim, we will be releasing him tomorrow morning." He looked at Caitlyn sternly. "That does not mean that something might not come up between now and then. We are still continuing with the investigation—speaking of which..." He turned back to James. "I wanted to ask you, Lord Fitzroy, about any new residents in the village."

"New residents?" James frowned. "Well, in terms of tenants, the two old workers' cottages on the edge of the main estate have recently been leased. They were refurbished earlier this year, with the intention of renting them out as short lets for weekends and on a weekly basis. A lot of Londoners like the idea of a 'holiday home' in the Cotswolds, you see, and this provides them with a way to indulge in that fantasy without the cost and hassles of buying and maintaining a second home."

"When did the new tenants arrive?"

"Both of them moved in last week. The larger cottage is rented to a Mrs Gertrude Smith; she's a widow—a middle-aged lady with a small terrier—"

"Oh! I think I might have met her," said Caitlyn. "Last night, just before the film began... there was a rather aggressive terrier that ran up to Bran and started trying to attack him."

"Yes, that would be Rocco," said James with a rueful laugh. "He seems to have taken a dislike to poor Bran and we've had quite a few skirmishes since they moved in. She has the cottage on a weekly basis, to be renewed each fortnight—I am not sure how long she intends to stay." His tone was neutral but Caitlyn got the distinct feeling that James was hoping Gertrude Smith and her belligerent terrier would decide to leave soon.

"And the other?" asked Inspector Walsh.

"The other cottage is rented to a young man called Lionel Spelling. He's an English teacher—he teaches in a language school in London—and he's taken the cottage for a month. I haven't seen much of him, to be honest. The estate agent handled all the details."

"Do you know if he was at the cinema last night?" asked Inspector Walsh.

"I didn't see him—but that doesn't mean that he wasn't there, of course," said James with a shrug. "I'm afraid there was such a large crowd and I wasn't particularly looking for him, so..."

"No matter. I shall speak to Mrs Smith and Mr Spelling in due course. We will be conducting a search of the cottages as well." The inspector looked towards the Manor. "And I believe that you also have a new member of staff, Lord Fitzroy? One of my men mentioned that."

James looked startled. "Yes, Giles Mosley, the new butler—but surely you don't suspect him? He came with excellent references."

"Anyone who is new to the village is of interest to me. When did Mr Mosley arrive?"

"The day before yesterday. Poor chap, it was in at the deep end for him. He barely had time to unpack before he was roped in to help with the preparations for yesterday's cinema event."

"So he was on the scene yesterday?"

"Oh yes. He was helping the staff set up on the lawn."

"Hmm..." Inspector Walsh stroked his moustache again thoughtfully. "I'd like to question him later."

CHAPTER SIX

An hour later, as the girls drove back towards Tillyhenge, Caitlyn was still mulling over the mystery of Pierre Rochat's murder. Was Inspector Walsh right about the "vampire" aspect of the murder simply being a cover—a way to distract from the real crime? Who would want to kill Rochat? And why?

A petulant "*Mew!*" from the wicker basket on her lap brought her out of her thoughts.

Pomona chuckled in the driver's seat next to her. "I don't think Nibs likes his new way of travel."

"Yes, I'm sure he'd prefer to ride loose, so he could get up to more mischief!" said Caitlyn. She looked affectionately at the little whiskered face peeking out through the bars of the carrier and wagged a finger at the kitten. "No more stowing away in Pomona's handbag, Nibs, or running up a tree and forcing me to break into the Manor to rescue you."

"What are you talking about?" asked Pomona.

Caitlyn laughed. "Okay, 'breaking into' is a bit of an exaggeration... Nibs climbed up a tree and jumped onto a window ledge at the back of the Manor and got stuck up there. I had to find a way in through an old locked door and up the back staircase to rescue him. I ended up in this creepy room trying to grab him from the inside of the window but he jumped off the ledge before I could reach him." Caitlyn shook her head at the memory. "I nearly had a heart attack until I saw that he was all right!"

But Pomona's attention had been caught by something else. "Creepy room? What creepy room?"

"Maybe creepy is the wrong word. It just had a sort of vibe... or maybe it was just the way it looked: everything was covered in white sheets. It's actually the Portrait Gallery and there are loads of oil portraits of the Fitzroys—James's ancestors—along one wall."

"What's under the white sheets?" asked Pomona.

"I don't know—I didn't look. Furniture, I guess. Maybe display cabinets? James told me that his father kept his occult collection in there."

Pomona took her eyes off the road to stare at her. "James? James's father? The old Lord Fitzroy? He was interested in magic and the occult?"

"Yes, he had an almost fanatical interest, apparently. It seems strange, doesn't it? I mean, James doesn't believe in the paranormal at all."

"Oh yeah, you can say that again! I was talking to him the other day and he told me that he broke up with a girlfriend in college 'cos she got, like, really obsessed with magic and witchcraft."

"Really?" Caitlyn looked at her, startled. "That seems a bit... extreme, doesn't it? I mean, I've heard him scoff at myths and superstitions sometimes, and I know he doesn't believe the village rumours about the Widow Mags being a witch, but I didn't think he'd break up with a girl just because she believes in magic."

"Well, you know, some things are just deal-breakers for some people... Like, I had this friend who would never go out with any guy who smoked. No matter how cute or rich or awesome he was, if he smoked—he was out. I kinda got the impression James feels the same way about people who are into magic and witchcraft and stuff. Anyway, this girlfriend sounded like a total nutcase. She was always, like, wanting him to go to Stonehenge with her and do magical rites at sunrise and stuff like that... Besides, if his dad was obsessive about it— maybe that turned him off too." Pomona shrugged.

Caitlyn digested all this in silence. She had to admit that, deep down inside, she had harboured a secret wish that she could tell James the truth about herself one day. But would he ever look at her the same way again if he discovered that she was a witch? She couldn't bear the thought of him recoiling from her in disgust or contempt.

When they arrived at *Bewitched by Chocolate*, however, all thought of James left her mind. There was the most incredible rich chocolatey fragrance coming from the kitchen at the back of the converted cottage. Caitlyn and Pomona walked in to find the Widow Mags standing at the central wooden table, surrounded by a variety of mixing bowls, baking trays, and ramekins.

The old witch glanced up. "About time," she snapped.

Caitlyn smiled to herself but said nothing. She had learned by now that her grandmother's bark was a lot worse than her bite. Beneath that gruff exterior was warm wisdom and a kind heart. She also wondered if the old witch might've been slightly peeved at her decision to stay at the Manor for the next few days. Proud and fiercely independent, the Widow Mags disliked admitting that she had any weakness or wanted anyone for company, but Caitlyn suspected that her grandmother had grown used to having her around.

It made Caitlyn feel warm inside to think that the cantankerous old witch actually missed her. She hadn't had an easy time since arriving in Tillyhenge. Well, discovering that you had an entire family on the other side of the world took a bit of getting used to—never mind finding out that you belonged to a family of witches! And if she had hoped to find a sweet cuddly old grandmother waiting to receive her with open arms, she had been sorely disappointed. The Widow Mags was blunt, cranky, and demanding, with a fierce appearance that reinforced her reputation as the "village witch". Oh, it wasn't her fault, of course, that nature had given her dark slashing eyebrows, a slightly hooked nose, and wild grey hair, which she usually pulled back into a messy bun, but it was easy to see why most of the village was afraid of her. And especially since they whispered that the chocolates in her shop were *bewitched*. Oh, they had to be, the local gossips insisted, because nothing could taste so mouth-wateringly delicious and make you feel so sinfully good without the help of magic...

The irony was, the chocolates *weren't* enchanted—they were simply very good. In addition to being a witch, the Widow Mags was also a skilled chocolatier and her delicious truffles, bonbons, and gourmet chocolate bars were out-of-this-world. Caitlyn hoped she would have her grandmother's talent one day; after all, working chocolate was in her blood. The witches in her family had inherited a special ability to tap into the ancient magic of *cacao* and Caitlyn had already seen glimpses of this in her own powers. *It would be nice if I could control those powers though*, she thought wryly, recalling what had happened with the children at the cinema.

"Did you hear what happened last night?" she

asked the Widow Mags.

"Yes," said the old witch grimly. "The news was all over the village this morning. Bertha came over first thing and told me." She gave Caitlyn a sharp look. "Heard the police arrested Viktor?"

"Yes, they've taken him to the station for questioning—he was found lurking near the body— but there isn't really any evidence to tie him to the murder. I spoke to the inspector this morning and I think they'll release him tomorrow."

"Good." The Widow Mags gave a nod.

Pomona had been holding a wriggling Nibs in her arms. Now she set the kitten down and came towards the wooden table. "Omigod! What's that amazing smell?" she asked, inhaling deeply.

"French chocolate soufflé," said the Widow Mags, whisking a spatula expertly around a bowl.

"Chocolate soufflé! My favourite! Can I taste one?"

"You'll have to make them first," said the Widow Mags. She pointed at some ceramic ramekins sitting on the table. "You can start by lining those with butter."

The two girls had barely sat down when the back door to the cottage opened and a lanky girl of eighteen walked in. Caitlyn broke into a smile at the sight of her English cousin, Evie. If the Widow Mags hadn't been the grandmother of her dreams, at least her aunt, Bertha—the Widow Mags's oldest daughter—was exactly like the warm, motherly figure she had always yearned for. And Bertha's daughter, Evie, was like the little sister she had never had.

Despite there only being four years between them, Caitlyn felt much older and quite protective towards the younger girl. Maybe it was because she could relate to Evie's awkwardness and lack of confidence. And she understood what it was like to be frustrated and embarrassed by your appearance. Together, she and Evie often looked wistfully at Pomona's easy grace and glamourous good looks, whilst they each struggled with their own demons: Caitlyn with her large hips and Evie with her frizzy red hair and teenage acne.

Today, however, Caitlyn was surprised to notice that Evie's complexion looked unusually good and the younger girl flushed with pleasure at her compliments.

"It's a spell," she confided in a whisper. "I found it in an old book in Mum's bedroom and tried it this morning."

"A spell?" said Pomona, exchanging a worried look with Caitlyn.

Evie's spells were known for one thing: ending in disaster. Although she was born and raised in a witch family, her magical skills were sadly lacking— something Caitlyn had learned the hard way when she first arrived in Tillyhenge and Evie's attempts to cure her headache ended in things sprouting out of her ears. She still winced at the memory of her reflection in the mirror.

Since then, she and Pomona had suffered through several of Evie's spells gone horrendously wrong. So now they both looked at the younger girl's clear, pink skin incredulously. Pomona leaned to one side and surreptitiously peered around Evie's back, as if checking for strange things growing out of her head.

"You used a spell to get rid of your pimples?" Caitlyn asked. "And it worked?"

"Yes, it was easy! Well, once I figured out how to aim better. I can do it for you too, if you like!" offered Evie. She stared at Caitlyn's forehead. "You've got a small zit on your temple—I can zap that and—"

"Uh... no, that's okay. Thanks anyway," said Caitlyn, quickly clamping a hand over her temple.

"Are you girls going to natter all day or are you going to help me with the chocolate soufflés?" asked the Widow Mags.

Hurriedly, Evie sat down at the table across from Caitlyn and Pomona, and all three girls picked up a ramekin each. Taking some fresh butter, they smeared it lightly on the inside of the small ceramic bowls. Then—following the Widow Mags's instructions—they sprinkled some granulated sugar on top, tilting and rolling the ramekins so that the sugar coated the inside surface with a glittering lining. Next, they watched as the old witch heated equal parts fresh milk and cream in a small cauldron over the fire, stirring it until it began to boil gently.

"Fetch me some dark chocolate from the pantry, the one with the highest cocoa content," directed the Widow Mags.

Pomona hurried to comply and brought back several dark brown slabs of smooth, glossy chocolate, which she carefully broke into chunks and added to the simmering cauldron. They all watched as the chocolate melted into the white liquid in beautiful dark swirls while the Widow Mags continued to stir slowly. Soon, the liquid in the cauldron had turned a dark, gleaming brown. The Widow Mags added a small bowl of pure, unsweetened cocoa powder—"For a more intense chocolatey flavour," she explained—followed by a bit of water. When the mixture was combined to her satisfaction, she took it off the heat and set it on the table to cool.

"Now for the most important part—the eggs," said the old witch, raising a hand.

"Wait, Grandma—I can get them for you!" said Evie. "I've been practising the Levitation spell all week!"

The Widow Mags looked doubtful. "Evie, I don't think—"

"No, no, I can do it!"

Before anyone could stop her, Evie stretched a hand towards the carton of eggs on the counter and chanted:

"Gravity defy,
Rise up and fly!"

The egg carton trembled, then the lid flipped open and two eggs rose shakily from their slots. They began to move jerkily through the air towards the wooden table. Caitlyn held her breath and everyone watched as the eggs floated across the room, with Evie directing them, her tongue stuck between her teeth in concentration. The eggs were almost at the table and Caitlyn was about to exhale in relief when one of them suddenly wobbled in mid-air, lurched sideways, and fell on the Widow Mags's head.

SPLAT!

There was a horrified silence as the three girls stared at the slimy yolk that had splattered down one side of the Widow Mags's hair.

"Oh!" Evie clamped a hand to her mouth. "Oh my Goddess! Grandma, I'm so sorry!"

The Widow Mags gave her a disgruntled look, then sighed and rose from the table. "I'm going to my room to clean up," she muttered.

After the old witch had left the kitchen, Evie slumped down in a chair. She looked so dejected that Caitlyn gave her arm a squeeze.

"Don't worry, Evie—it was an accident."

"I thought I'd mastered the Levitation spell," said Evie miserably. "I'm never going to be any good as a witch..."

"Of course, you are! You were almost there—it was just a slip at the last moment."

"Yeah, I'm sure if you tried it again, you'd do it, no problem," said Pomona, giving the younger girl an encouraging smile. "Maybe with something other than eggs though," she added hastily.

Evie brightened. "Okay! I'll try again with this."

She reached out and picked up a ramekin, placing it on the table in front of her. Then she furrowed her brow in concentration and stretched her hand towards the little ceramic bowl. Once again, she chanted:

"Gravity defy,
Rise up and fly!"

The ramekin trembled, then tilted so that one side lifted off the table... before thumping back down again.

"Maybe try with something lighter?" Caitlyn suggested.

Evie looked around and spied the Widow Mags's reading spectacles lying next to a mixing bowl. She stretched a hand towards them and chanted the spell again. Everyone held their breath. The spectacles shifted slightly, then slid along the table, gathering speed until they launched themselves into the air like a miniature airplane taking off from a runway.

"Holy guacamole! You did it!" cried Pomona, looking up in wonder as the spectacles zoomed around her head.

They flew like a giant insect—a sort of dragonfly, perhaps—with the two lenses as glass wings on either side. Nibs the kitten looked up with interest, then scampered after the spectacles, running in circles around the room as they flapped above his head.

"That is so cool!" said Pomona. "I wish I could do magic. Then I'd never have to find my sunglasses again—I could just get them to, like, fly to me!"

"Maybe you'd better bring them back down now," said Caitlyn, glancing nervously at the kitchen doorway. The Widow Mags would probably return any moment and she didn't think the old witch would find the sight of her reading glasses zooming around the kitchen so amusing.

Evie waved a hand towards the spectacles and chanted:

"Gravity obey,
To earth you must stay."

Nothing happened. The Widow Mags's glasses kept flying in circles above their heads.

"Gravity obey, / To earth you must stay!" said Evie, louder this time.

The spectacles soared upwards, then dived down like a swooping bird. Everyone gasped as they narrowly missed the corner of the table before swerving up again.

"*Meew!*" cried Nibs, leaping up in the air to try and catch them.

"Okay, I think this is getting a bit out of control," said Pomona. "Better get them back before they break a lens."

"I'm... I'm trying!" said Evie, an edge of panic in her voice. She stretched both hands towards the flying spectacles and shouted: "*GRAVITY OBEY, / TO EARTH YOU MUST STAY!*"

The spectacles zoomed past her, doing a loop in mid-air. It looked almost as if they were taunting her. Pomona made a grab but the glasses swerved and darted away.

"Oh no you don't!" she shouted, chasing after them. "I'm going to catch you if it's the last thing I do!"

The spectacles zigzagged right and left, then made a beeline for the open window.

"Pomie! The window!" Caitlyn gasped.

Pomona made a wild lunge but wasn't fast enough. The spectacles swerved upwards, then soared out between the open panes.

"Nooo!" cried Evie.

She rushed to the back door and flung it open, running out into the garden behind the cottage. The other two girls followed, but it was too late. By the time they reached the back gate, the spectacles were already flitting into the forest, disappearing from sight between the trees.

"Oh nooo.... What am I going to tell Grandma?" asked Evie, clutching her face.

"Maybe they'll come back later on their own," suggested Caitlyn.

"No, they won't," moaned Evie. "They've gone feral now."

"Well, maybe you should be proud," said Pomona brightly. "Instead of a life of drudgery perched on the Widow Mags's nose, you've set them free! Maybe they'll meet their own kind in the wild and make spectacle babies."

Caitlyn rolled her eyes and Evie didn't look amused.

"What am I going to tell Grandma?" she asked again.

"Maybe she won't notice," said Pomona hopefully.

The words had barely left her mouth when a grey-haired figure with a dowager's hump appeared in the rear cottage doorway.

"What are you girls doing out there?" demanded the Widow Mags. "And where have my reading glasses gone?"

CHAPTER SEVEN

Both Caitlyn and Evie froze, their mouths hanging open and their expressions panicked.

"Reading glasses? What reading glasses?" asked Pomona brightly.

"I left my spectacles on the kitchen table. They're gone now. One of you must have moved them— unless they've gone walking by themselves," said the Widow Mags suspiciously.

Evie gulped.

The old witch fixed Caitlyn with a steely gaze. "Have you seen them?"

"I... er..." Caitlyn stammered. She knew she should just make something up but she found it hard to look her grandmother straight in the eye and lie.

Pomona, however, had no such problems. "I

didn't see any glasses on the table. Are you sure you left them there?" she asked glibly. "Maybe you left them somewhere else and forgot. I do that kinda thing all the time, you know. Like... I'd be so sure I parked my car on Level One at the mall, and actually it was on Level Five. Anyway, they'll turn up sometime. C'mon! Let's keep going with the soufflés. So what are we gonna do with the eggs?"

As she chattered, Pomona put an arm around the Widow Mags's shoulders and hustled the old woman back into the cottage. Caitlyn and Evie exchanged looks of admiration and followed. A few minutes later, they were standing at the table again, cracking several eggs and separating the whites from the yolks. The Widow Mags took the yolks and mixed them slowly into the chocolate, whilst the girls followed her directions and beat the egg whites with some sugar.

"Man, don't you have electric mixers here?" complained Pomona after several moments of vigorous beating. She dropped her whisk and flexed her bicep. "My arm is killing me!"

"I could make the whisks move by themselves using magic!" said Evie. "Do you want me to enchant them and—"

"NO!" said Caitlyn and Pomona together.

Pomona snatched up her whisk and began beating again. "You know what? On second thought, this is good exercise."

Finally, the egg whites were whipped into light,

fluffy peaks and folded carefully into the chocolate mixture, which they poured into the ramekins waiting on a baking tray.

"Oooh, they smell so good..." Pomona hovered over the tray. "Do we have to bake them? Can't we just, like, have them like this?"

She poked a finger towards the nearest ramekin but the Widow Mags slapped her hand away with mock ferocity.

"Patience, girl," she growled. "You can taste them when they've risen."

She lifted the tray and placed it in the pre-heated oven. Within minutes, a heavenly aroma began to fill the kitchen and Caitlyn became almost as impatient as Pomona to taste the finished soufflés! They took turns peering through the oven window and watching as the chocolate batter slowly rose, forming little mounds above the rims of the ramekins. Finally, the Widow Mags decided that the soufflés had baked long enough and took the tray out.

"Omigod! Omigod! The *smell*!" Pomona took a long, exaggerated sniff and clutched her heart. "I'm gonna die if I don't taste some!"

The Widow Mags chuckled and held up a hand. "Wait. There is one last step."

"What?" asked Pomona, clutching a spoon and hopping from foot to foot.

The Widow Mags took a handful of icing sugar from a special container and held it out in the palm of her hand. She blew on it gently. The powdered sugar billowed out in a sparkling white cloud, which settled on top of the chocolate soufflés like a dusting of pure white snow. Caitlyn remembered seeing her grandmother do something similar before—when the old witch had made her chocolate fudge cake masterpiece for the Fitzroy Summer Garden Party.

Pomona grabbed one of the ramekins and stuck her spoon eagerly into the top. The thin crispy crust, which had caramelised over the soufflé, cracked and molten chocolate oozed out. Pomona scooped up a generous spoonful and stuck it into her mouth.

"Ohhh..." She sighed and her eyes rolled into the back of her head. "Omigod... I think I've died and gone to heaven..." She scooped up another spoonful and thrust it at Caitlyn. "Man, you gotta taste this! It's so light and fluffy—but sort of rich and soft and gooey at the same time... it's like... pure chocolate heaven!"

Caitlyn laughed and took the spoon. As the intense flavour of the moist, rich chocolate filled her mouth, she had to admit that Pomona was right. The soufflé was absolutely heavenly. She passed the ramekin to Evie, who also sighed with pleasure as she tasted a mouthful.

"*Meew!*" said Nibs as he watched from a chair next to them. He put out an inquisitive paw.

"Sorry, Nibs, you can't have any—it's chocolate

and that's poisonous to cats," said Caitlyn.

"I'd better put the rest out in the shop before you girls eat them all," growled the Widow Mags, but Caitlyn could see from the smile twitching at the corners of her mouth that she was pleased by their reactions.

"Wait... how are you gonna sell them in the shop?" asked Pomona. "I mean, don't soufflés collapse when they cool down? I thought that was the whole thing with them—like, you have to eat them fresh as soon as they come out of the oven."

"Ah..." The Widow Mags nodded towards the other ramekins. "That's what the sugar was for."

"The sugar?" Pomona glanced at the remaining soufflés, which all still looked as perfect as when they had come straight out of the oven. "But lots of soufflés have powdered sugar on top—"

"Not powdered sugar like mine," said the Widow Mags with a smile. "It is the finest confectioners' sugar, mixed with a little bit of... well, you can call it 'fairy dust'. It places a charm on the soufflés, preserving them perfectly as they are—until it comes time to eat them. So they won't sink and deflate like normal soufflés."

She picked up the tray and led the way to the front of the cottage, where she opened up the chocolate shop for business. Caitlyn stood and looked around the store with pleasure: it was so different compared to when she had first arrived in Tillyhenge! Then, it had been dark and ominous, with peeling paint and dusty cobwebs festooning the corners. Now it was clean and freshly painted, with attractive shelving and a large window display showing an assortment of chocolate truffles and bonbons, as well as some of the intricate chocolate sculptures that the Widow Mags had created. A few tables and chairs had also been arranged in the corners of the room, so that customers could sit down and order a slice of decadent chocolate fudge cake or a mug of rich hot cocoa. (And once they had a taste, they usually bought more to take home or give to friends and family!)

Caitlyn glanced at Pomona with a smile. It was all her doing, really: her bubbly American cousin had somehow cajoled a recalcitrant Widow Mags into letting her do a "makeover" for the store and the results had been amazing. Within a day, many more tourists had started to venture down the village's back lane into *Bewitched by Chocolate,* and business was growing.

If only we could say the same of the villagers, thought Caitlyn with an inward sigh. Although a few had befriended the Widow Mags, most of the local residents still viewed the old witch with fear and suspicion, and snubbed her "enchanted" chocolate shop. It made Caitlyn seethe with frustration, especially when she tasted some of the terrible chocolates on sale in shops nearby.

Still, there's hope—even if it means winning the villagers over one at a time, thought Caitlyn as she saw six-year-old Molly Jenkins run into the shop, towing her mother behind her. Only a month ago, the little girl would never have been allowed to set foot in the shop, never mind taste any of the chocolates. But when the Widow Mags saved the little girl's life recently, Beth, her mother, was so grateful that she put aside all her prejudices about witchcraft and magic. Since then, she had become a regular at *Bewitched by Chocolate*, bringing Molly to sample the delicious truffles and other chocolate candy.

"Ooh, something smells fantastic!" said Beth, inhaling appreciatively.

"We've just baked some chocolate soufflés," said Caitlyn, gesturing to the tray on the counter. "Would you like one?"

"Actually, we came because Molly has been very good and I promised her I'd let her choose a chocolate treat."

"I want that one!" cried Molly, pointing a chubby finger at a truffle with velvety chocolate ganache covered with freshly roasted, chopped hazelnuts.

"What's the magic word?" asked Beth sternly.

Molly gave the Widow Mags a gap-toothed smile. "Please?"

The old witch looked indulgently at the little girl. "You can choose more than one."

"Okay, I want that one too," said Molly, pointing to a milk chocolate truffle with a salty-sweet peanut-butter centre. "And that one! With the strawberry. Please," she added belatedly.

"And that will be quite enough," said Beth with a smile. "Otherwise you'll ruin your appetite." She opened her purse, then eyed the tray of chocolate soufflés longingly. "My, those look so delicious..."

"You gotta have one!" said Pomona, picking up a ramekin and thrusting it towards the other woman.

Beth laughed weakly. "Oh, I really shouldn't... I'm supposed to be watching the calories..." She hesitated as the rich aroma of chocolate wafted up from the ramekin. "Oh... go on, then!" she said suddenly with a chuckle. "My diet can start tomorrow."

"What you need with that is some fresh whipped cream," said the Widow Mags, lifting a bowl from behind the counter and spooning a generous dollop onto the soufflé. They all watched in anticipation as Beth dipped a spoon into the ramekin and took a mouthful of the dark chocolate soufflé and the snowy white cream.

"Mmm... oh, this is absolutely amazing!" she cried. "I've never tasted chocolate soufflé like this! It's as if you're eating a mouthful of cloud... and yet it has such a rich chocolatey flavour... Can I buy one to take home? It might mollify Hubby a bit," she explained with a smile. "He's a bit put out as me and Molly didn't get home until very late last night. We were held up at the Manor..."

She glanced quickly at Molly to see if her daughter was listening but the little girl had wandered off with Evie to look at some chocolate sculptures on the other side of the shop.

Beth lowered her voice. "The police wanted to check everyone before they let us go home, in case we'd had some contact with the murdered man. Did you hear? They say he was killed by a vampire! There were fang marks on his neck!" She gave a delicious shudder, then looked at Caitlyn and Pomona. "You girls were there last night. Did you see the body?"

"Yes, I did," Caitlyn admitted.

"Was there a lot of blood?"

"No, there wasn't, actually. I didn't see any blood."

"Another mark of a vampire attack," said Beth, nodding her head. "They would have sucked all the blood out, see? That's why you couldn't see any! I heard that the murdered man was as white as a ghost—not a drop of blood left in him!"

"He *was* pale, but I don't think it was any different from a 'normal' dead person," protested Caitlyn. She was starting to get annoyed at the way things were twisted and exaggerated by the rumour mill.

"Oh no, it wasn't normal," Beth insisted. "Anyway, I heard that they might have got the murderer! The police have him locked up in a cell down at the station. Some nasty old man... strange, I never thought vampires were old men..." She gave another exaggerated shudder. "I do hope it's him—

otherwise it means there's still a vampire killer running loose!"

"What a load o' crock," came a new voice and they looked up to see a tall wiry man with greying hair and a good-looking, weather-beaten face come into the store. It was Jeremy Bottom, one of the local farmers who ran a small organic dairy farm. He stomped up to the counter in his heavy rubber boots and grinned at the assembled women.

"You're not believing all that talk, Beth? You sound like my sister, Vera," he said, shaking his head in disgust. "Spending all her time with the village gossips down at the post office shop... Like I keep telling her, there's no vampire killer on the loose."

"How do you explain the puncture marks on the dead man's neck then?" Beth demanded. "Those are obviously made by fangs!"

Jeremy shrugged. "Maybe it was an animal. Or maybe 'twas a weapon sharpened to look like fangs. I'm glad Inspector Walsh is a sensible man and doesn't listen to all this hysterical speculation. I saw him this morning by the village pub and he reckons it's someone pretending to be a vampire."

Beth looked unconvinced. "Why would anyone want to pretend to be a vampire?"

Jeremy shrugged again. "Who knows how them criminal minds work...?" He paused, then added with a dark look, "If you ask me, the police should be questioning that young chap who's moved into one o' those workers' cottages—you know, the ones that have just been done up."

"The English teacher?" said Beth, frowning. "Yes, he *is* very odd, isn't he?"

"What do you mean?" asked Caitlyn.

Beth made a face. "He always wears black—even his lips are painted black! And his skin is so pale... I wondered if he was ill or something. Yesterday, I saw him in the village and he was wearing a weird black leather vest with buckles all over it... *And* he's got an earring," she added, as if that clinched it.

"Sounds like he's kinda got a Goth thing going," said Pomona with a grin. "Lots of people dress like that. It's just, like, a fashion statement, you know."

"Well, he's not very friendly either," complained Beth. "When I saw him yesterday, it was in the village post shop and everyone was trying to be friendly-like, but he hardly said a word!"

Caitlyn wasn't sure she could blame Lionel Spelling. She could remember her own experience of going into the village post office shop for the first time. Like any small village, Tillyhenge thrived on gossip and the locals' curiosity towards newcomers could be overwhelming. She could just imagine the resident old ladies pouncing on the hapless young teacher and trying to pump him for information.

"Maybe he's just shy," she suggested.

Beth snorted. "Not likely! I think he's hiding something."

Jeremy nodded his agreement. "There's

something very dodgy about that Spelling chap. Wouldn't be surprised if he was mixed up in this murder—"

He broke off suddenly as a young man walked into the shop and Caitlyn realised that it was the very person they had been talking about: Lionel Spelling.

CHAPTER EIGHT

The young English teacher really was very pale—like someone who hadn't seen the sun for months—although this might have partly been due to the fact that his hair had been dyed very, very black, which contrasted sharply—and unflatteringly—with his milky white complexion. Despite the heat of the summer's day, he was wearing a black long-sleeved silk shirt with a ruffled collar, and black leather trousers with buckles down the side seams. He looked slightly ridiculous, like he had come off the set of a fantasy movie, and Caitlyn had to make an effort not to stare.

He hesitated on the threshold as he saw them all standing around the counter and looked as if he would turn around again and leave, but Pomona sprang forwards.

"Hi! You're new to the village, aren't you? I'm Pomona," she said, giving him a dazzling smile.

The young man blinked and Caitlyn chuckled to herself. When Pomona turned on the charm, most men were putty in her hands and it looked like Lionel Spelling was no exception.

"Ramona?" he said.

"No, Pomona... like the Roman goddess of fruits." She grinned and waved an airy hand. "Yeah. It's different. My mom was, like, going through this mythology phase. Anyway, what's your name?"

"Um... Lionel... Lionel Spelling," he mumbled. He had an unusually high-pitched, feminine voice. He glanced at the group gathered around the counter again, especially at Beth and Jeremy, who were eyeing him suspiciously, and shifted uncomfortably. "I... I think I'd better go—"

Pomona reached out and fingered the fabric of his sleeve. "That's a cool outfit! Is it from Camden Market in London? I had this friend who was really into Goth fashion and she used to get the best stuff from there."

"Yes, it is, actually," he said, a note of pleasant surprise in his voice. He relaxed slightly. "I get a lot of my clothes from there. Well, not my work clothes, of course," he said, flushing slightly. "I don't dress like this when I'm teaching."

"Sure," said Pomona. "But school's over and it's the summer vacation, right? So it's your personal time now—you know, let your hair down a bit." She grinned and looked at his longish haircut. "Literally."

Lionel Spelling grinned as well, thawing even more. "Yes, it's nice to not have to worry about setting an example all the time. As a teacher, you get a lot of that, you know."

"Yeah, I'll bet! People are, like, so judgemental, aren't they? They judge you based on the clothes you wear and the hairstyle you have and the car you drive and the movies you watch... speaking of which," said Pomona smoothly. "Can you believe what happened at the Open-Air Cinema last night?"

Lionel Spelling stiffened. "The cinema? No, I... I mean, I wasn't there. I stayed in my cottage all night. I only heard about the murder this morning."

Pomona made a face of exaggerated surprise. "You didn't go? Why not? Everyone at the village was there!"

"I just... I fancied staying in last night."

Pomona gave him an arch look. "Ooh... snuggling with a girlfriend?"

The young teacher flushed again. "No, I was alone." He shifted uncomfortably and said, "Look, it's been nice chatting to you but I'd better go now—"

"Oh, but aren't you gonna get any chocolates?" said Pomona.

"Maybe some other time," said Lionel Spelling. Then, before Pomona could say another word, he turned and hurried out of the shop, disappearing down the lane.

As soon as he was out of earshot, Jeremy Bottom exclaimed, "There! What did I tell you? Guilty as sin, he is!"

"What do you mean?" asked Caitlyn.

"He said he was alone, which means he doesn't have one o' them things—you know, 'alibis'. He could have been anywhere last night... like sneaking through the forest, looking for his next victim!"

Beth realised suddenly that Molly had come back and was now standing, wide-eyed, listening to the adults' conversation. Quickly, she said, "But that's just in the storybook, isn't it, Jeremy? I'm sure they all lived happily ever after. Anyway, we'd best be off now. Say thank you for the chocolates," she instructed her daughter.

"Thank you!" said Molly, clutching her treats and beaming at the Widow Mags. Then, impulsively, she threw her arms around the old woman's waist and gave her a hug. "You're my favouritest witch!"

The Widow Mags looked speechless and the rest of the group didn't know whether to laugh or pretend politely that they hadn't heard.

"You're welcome... Come back any time," said the old witch gruffly, clearing her throat.

"I'd better be going too," said Jeremy Bottom as the mother and daughter left the shop. "I only came in to get some o' those..." He pointed to a bag of chocolate-covered raisins and grinned. "Got a bit of an addiction to 'em. And that son o' mine likes 'em too. By the way, Evie..." He turned to the teenage girl who had been standing quietly in the background. "I've been wanting to thank you for helping Chris."

"M-me?" said Evie.

"Yes, the poor lad was suffering from hayfever something chronic... but ever since he saw you at your mother's herbal store a couple o' weeks ago, he's been completely cured. Whatever you did to him, it's worked a treat." He beamed at her.

Evie had gone bright red. "Oh... er... I'm... I'm glad."

Jeremy made a puzzled face. "Only funny thing is, he's developed a real liking for carrots—keeps munching 'em all the time now—we're going through kilos o' the stuff! And he always used to hate 'em. Don't suppose you know why? Is it like a side-effect o' the stuff you gave him?"

"I... um..." Evie looked slightly panicked. "I'm not sure..."

Caitlyn came to her rescue. "How's Ferdinand?" she asked loudly.

The farmer's face creased into a smile at the mention of his bull. "Oh, he's doing great! Still sweet as ever, of course, and loves a bit o' a cuddle... but he's so much happier now, spending his time with the herd." He scratched his head. "Still don't understand how the girls just took to him like that, all of a sudden, when they wouldn't even look at him before. Nature's a mystery, eh?" He gave a good-natured shrug. "Anyway, it's been great for me and the growth o' the farm, I can tell you. In fact, the vet's just been out this week and he reckons there's a good chance we'll have some 'Ferdinand babies' in spring next year," he chuckled.

Pomona squealed. "Ooh, baby cows! I can't wait to see them!"

CHAPTER NINE

The chocolate soufflés were a huge hit, and within an hour they were all sold out. The Widow Mags retreated to the kitchen to make more, leaving Caitlyn and Pomona to look after the shop whilst Evie took on the task of ferrying each batch of freshly baked soufflés from the kitchen. The girls were surprised to find that business was brisk—it seemed that visitors who had come to Tillyhenge for the cinema last night had also heard about its unusual chocolate shop, and curiosity had prompted many to return.

"Jeez, people are so nosy," said Pomona as she finished serving a customer. "Did you hear that guy? He wanted to know if I saw the body last night and if there was, like, blood everywhere. And he wasn't even there himself—he lives in Cheltenham and just came to Tillyhenge today 'cos he heard all the gossip about the murder." She picked up the empty soufflé tray and headed towards the door connecting the shop to the back of the cottage. "I'm gonna get some more soufflés—I hope they've got some ready."

She had barely disappeared when a new customer entered *Bewitched by Chocolate*. Caitlyn felt a flash of delight as she recognised Antoine de Villiers. The handsome Frenchman sauntered up to the counter, his eyes lighting up as he saw Caitlyn.

"*Quelle surprise!* Caitlyn—" he pronounced it "*Kat-lan*" in his charming French accent, "—this is an unexpected pleasure! I had not realised that you worked in this *chocolaterie*?"

Caitlyn smiled. "Well, I don't really... it belongs to my grandmother and I'm just helping out."

His eyes fell on the tray of soufflés on the counter and he gave another exclamation.

"*Ah, bon!* You have made the chocolate soufflé—the classic dessert of France. It is a special welcome for me, is it not?" He gave her saucy smile.

Caitlyn laughed. "No, I'm afraid it had nothing to do with you. My grandmother just decided to try out a new chocolate treat to sell in the shop."

"*Alors*, they are *magnifique*," said Antoine, looking at the soufflés with admiration. "It is not easy to make the perfect chocolate soufflé; they must be rich and creamy but also light and full of air. Hence the name: from the French verb *souffler*—'to puff up', you know? But it is something even the best restaurants often struggle with, a Holy Grail for many chefs... Your *grand-mère* must have great skill, eh?"

Caitlyn smiled. "Yes, she has a way with chocolate. Would you like one?"

He raised a teasing eyebrow. "With such beautiful eyes looking at me, *mademoiselle,* how can I say no?"

It was so ridiculous and over-the-top that Caitlyn laughed.

"You have a very lovely laugh," he said. "It is like the sound of bells ringing on a spring morning."

She didn't know whether to laugh even more at his flowery language or be touched by his poetic description. Okay, so it was cheesy—but she had to admit that a part of her quite liked it. She'd never been the object of such blatant admiration from a man before. And she was also enjoying the fact that—unlike with James Fitzroy—she didn't get horribly tongue-tied and self-conscious. In fact, she even felt brave enough to flirt a little in return. They were still laughing, leaning comfortably together against the counter, when Pomona came back from the kitchen. She stopped short at the sight of them.

Hastily, Caitlyn straightened and said, "Antoine, you remember my cousin, Pomona?"

"*Bien sûr*—who could forget such loveliness?"

Pomona gave him a cool look and a nod. Caitlyn was surprised. It wasn't like her cousin to respond in such an aloof manner to a man—especially a man as handsome as Antoine de Villiers. Still, she retreated slightly to let them talk. Now that Pomona was here, she half-expected Antoine to ignore her anyway—that was usually what happened whenever men met her cousin. Compared with Pomona's glamorous looks and easy confidence, Caitlyn usually didn't stand a chance.

But to her surprise, Antoine did not ignore her. Instead, he turned back and continued to flirt with her. Caitlyn was flattered—she had never had a man choose her over her cousin—and she felt herself blushing with a mixture of embarrassment and pleasure. Pomona stood and watched them for a moment, her mouth pressed into a thin line, then excused herself abruptly and headed back to the kitchen. As she was going through the connecting door, a little black ball of fluff slipped out and scampered up to the counter.

"Nibs, you really shouldn't be out here," said Caitlyn with mock sternness. "We can't have you getting under the customers' feet."

Antoine de Villiers looked down at the kitten, who had trotted over to him and was now sitting at his feet, staring up with big yellow eyes.

"*Meew!*" said Nibs, reaching up and hooking his claws into Antoine's trouser leg.

The Frenchman laughed as he reached down to disengage the kitten. "Ah, he has spirit, this one. He will be a little tiger when he is grown, *n'est-ce pas?*"

"Oh gosh, I hope not," said Caitlyn. "He causes enough trouble already at the size he is!" She gestured to the glass counter. "Would you like to sample some of the truffles?"

Antoine waved a hand. "Not now. But I will take a box as a gift back to the Manor—a small 'thank you' for having me as a guest. Perhaps you can wrap it for me?"

"Oh, sure," said Caitlyn, reaching below the counter and taking out a shallow giftbox, which she proceeded to fill with chocolate truffles. When it was full, she placed the lid over it, then found a length of gold ribbon to tie around it.

Nibs had jumped up on the counter and had been watching her curiously. Now he meowed excitedly at the sight of the ribbon and pounced, trying to grab the ends with his claws.

"No, Nibs..." Caitlyn frowned, flicking the ribbon out of the way.

The movement only excited the kitten more and he pounced again. He missed the ribbon but his claws caught the side of Caitlyn's bare arm, leaving a long scratch on her skin.

"*Ouch!*" cried Caitlyn, jerking back. She looked down ruefully. It was a shallow wound but bright red blood was already welling up along the length of the scratch.

There was a sound from across the counter and she looked up to see Antoine de Villiers staring fixedly at her arm. He had gone very pale and she could see beads of sweat forming on his forehead.

"It's only a scratch," she assured him. "It's not serious."

Antoine swallowed convulsively and clamped a hand over his mouth.

"Hey... are you all right?" she asked, reaching out to touch his arm.

He twitched. "I... The sight of blood disturbs me," he muttered, looking away.

"Oh. Sorry."

Caitlyn grabbed a napkin and wiped the red drops from her arm, then rummaged through the drawer below the counter until she found a First Aid kit. The Frenchman stood awkwardly, keeping his eyes averted, until she had covered the scratch with a bandage.

He cleared his throat. "*Pardon...* I should have offered my assistance but the blood... ever since I was a child, it is something which I—"

"Oh, no, no problem," said Caitlyn. "I totally understand. A lot of people are squeamish about blood, aren't they? In fact, my adoptive mother had a chauffeur who used to faint if he ever saw blood. It was quite extreme. I remember him telling me all about it; he said it's something to do with a primitive reflex in your brain—"

"Yes, yes," said Antoine quickly, obviously not wanting to talk about his embarrassing weakness. "It is not a great affliction. I certainly do not faint."

Caitlyn smiled to herself. "No, well... anyway,

here's your box of chocolates." She finished tying the ribbon and pushed the gift-wrapped box across the counter towards him.

"*Merci.*" He took the chocolates and gave her a smirk, back to his suave, confident self. "You will be returning to the Manor soon? Perhaps I can escort you?"

"No, we're not going back until quite late tonight. Pomona and I are having dinner with my grandmother."

"Ah, *quelle dommage...* it is a shame. I had hoped to continue our delightful conversation at dinner tonight."

Once again, Caitlyn felt a rush of pleasure at his desire for her company. "We'll be there tomorrow night," she promised. "I heard that James's friends are arriving from London and he's having a big meal."

"I shall look forward to that greatly," said Antoine de Villiers, grasping her hand and bringing it briefly to his lips. "*À demain, mademoiselle.*"

CHAPTER TEN

Caitlyn enjoyed the warm family atmosphere during dinner with the Widow Mags, her aunt Bertha, and Evie, but she noticed that Pomona seemed unusually quiet. Later, as they drove back to the Manor in silence, Caitlyn glanced at her cousin.

"Pomie… is something the matter?"

"No, nothing," said Pomona. Then she burst out, "You'd better watch yourself with that French guy."

"Antoine?" Caitlyn looked at her in surprise. "What do you mean?"

"He's way too much for you to handle."

"What's that supposed to mean?" asked Caitlyn with a flicker of irritation.

Pomona tossed her head. "I know guys, okay? He might have a fancy accent and a castle in France but Antoine de Villiers has 'bad boy' written all over him."

"How can you say that when you barely know him? And anyway, I thought you liked 'bad boys'."

"That's me. It's different for you."

"Why is it different for me?" Caitlyn felt her temper really rising. "Do you think I'm some kind of idiot?"

"No—you're just too sweet and innocent for a guy like Antoine de Villiers. Leave him to someone who knows how to handle men."

"You mean someone like you?" asked Caitlyn, stung.

Pomona shrugged. "Hey, I'm not interested in him... but I *have* dated a lot of guys whereas you—well, you haven't really dated *anyone*, have you?"

Caitlyn flushed. "Well, I... that doesn't mean I'm not a good judge of character!"

"But you're not," said Pomona flatly. "At least where men are concerned. You were, like, getting all pink and fluttery just 'cos he fed you a couple of clichés about how beautiful you looked. You were totally blinded by his charm."

"That's not true!" cried Caitlyn, angry and embarrassed. "I think you're just jealous!"

"Jealous? Me?"

"Yes! Because you're so used to guys always paying *you* the attention, and for once a man was interested in me instead. Your ego can't take it."

"Oh, gimme a break!" said Pomona, rolling her

eyes. "I'm not jealous! I'm saying this 'cos I care about you and don't wanna see you get hurt."

"*You're* the one who's always telling me I should flirt more," Caitlyn snapped. "You're always pushing me onto James—"

"James Fitzroy is different! He's a complete gentleman; he's noble and decent and would never take advantage of you—"

"I suppose you think I can only handle guys who are safe and boring," said Caitlyn bitterly.

"You think James is boring?"

"No," said Caitlyn quickly, feeling ashamed. "That's not what I meant. It's just... he's... well, he's so reserved. You never know what he's thinking or if he really likes you..."

"He's English! They're like that. You know, they feel a lot but don't show it on the outside. It's all, like, understatement with them. Okay, so you're not gonna get James showering you with compliments all the time—but he really cares for you. Like, big time."

"How do you know Antoine doesn't really care for me?" demanded Caitlyn. "Just because he makes it obvious doesn't mean he's not serious. Maybe he's just better at showing his feelings."

Pomona rolled her eyes again. "Honey, guys like Antoine de Villiers love seducing shy, innocent virgins. It's the ultimate game for them: the thrill of the chase. That French dude doesn't really care for you—he just wants to get you into his bed."

Caitlyn gasped and spluttered. "That's not true! You don't know Antoine at all... Anyway... I... I'm not a child! I'm old enough to look after myself and I don't need you to babysit me!"

"Fine!" snapped Pomona. "If you wanna be like that, then do what you want!"

Caitlyn turned away and stared furiously out of the window as they drove in silence back to the Manor. When they arrived, the grounds were dark, with only a few security lights on. It was nearly midnight and the household had obviously gone to bed. Caitlyn got out of the car, still seething, grabbed her holdall and slammed the passenger door harder than necessary. Pomona did the same and both girls stalked up the front steps, not looking at each other. They maintained a stony silence as they returned to the guestroom they shared and got into bed without saying goodnight.

When Caitlyn awoke the next morning, it took her a moment to remember what had happened and she felt her temper rising again as she recalled Pomona's words. She glanced across to the other bed and saw her cousin's blonde head buried amongst the pillows. Although there was no movement, somehow she had a feeling the other girl wasn't sleeping.

It wasn't their first fight, of course. Being more like sisters than cousins, they'd had their fair share of sibling arguments over the years, but in the past it was always Caitlyn who caved in first. She would apologise, and then Pomona would immediately apologise too, since she was usually just waiting for Caitlyn to make the first move.

Now Caitlyn looked at the blonde head turned away from hers and knew that Pomona was probably listening, waiting for her to speak. But for once, Caitlyn dug her heels in. Why should she apologise? She wasn't sorry for what she'd said yesterday! Instead, she got out of bed and washed and dressed quickly. When she came out of the bathroom, Pomona was still buried under the covers. Caitlyn hesitated, then set her lips and turned towards the door, leaving the room without a word to her cousin.

She went downstairs and let herself out of the main door, pausing at the top of the front steps to look around. The sky was a clear, washed blue and it looked as if it was going to be another lovely summer's day. She could see various members of staff going around the house and grounds, cleaning and tidying before the Manor officially opened to the public, and she wondered where James was. Probably out having an early morning ride or taking Bran for a walk before breakfast. And Antoine de Villiers? Probably in bed, Caitlyn thought with a wry smile. The Frenchman didn't look like the type to embrace early mornings.

She decided to go for a walk herself and wandered into the rose gardens that stretched out on one side of the Manor. Slowly, she strolled along the wide avenue between the rose beds, admiring the rambling bushes covered in exquisite deep-cupped blooms, in soft pastel shades of apricot, peach, and cream, with the occasional burst of salmon pink or vivid strawberry. The lovely fragrance of roses filled the air around her and she felt as if she had stepped into a romantic fairy tale. The enchanted rose garden, perhaps, in "Beauty and the Beast", where Belle's father had stolen a rose and been captured by the Beast...

As she came to the end of the avenue, she paused by a magnificent rosebush with huge, chalice-shaped blooms, each displaying dozens of velvety petals in a beautiful shade of creamy apricot. She leaned towards it, burying her nose in a fragrant blossom.

"Mind the mulch," said a voice.

She started and turned around to see Old Palmer, the Manor's Head Gardener, standing behind her. She followed his gaze and saw that she had stepped into the rose bed by mistake.

"Oh, sorry," she said, taking a hasty step back. She gave the old man a smile. "It's so beautiful, I forgot myself. I've never seen roses like these before—what are they? They look so different from the roses you get at the florist. Those have got thin, narrow flowers—these are so deep and full, and have so many petals."

"Pah! Those hybrid tea roses ye get in shops..." said the old gardener with great disdain. "Feeble, spindly things, always getting fungus and whatnot, and not even a whiff of fragrance... I'd never have those in my garden! No, *these* are real roses," he said, waving a proud hand towards the flowers around them. "Proper English roses: lots o' big flowers on a healthy bush... and smell the perfume!"

He cupped a blossom gently and tilted it towards Caitlyn, who obediently took a sniff. It was gorgeous: a warm tea fragrance, with hints of spiced apple and cloves.

"Ohhh...!" sighed Caitlyn. "I'd forgotten what roses could smell like! In fact, these remind me so much of the flowers you see in oil paintings... Are these like the antique roses that used to grow in castles in medieval times? I was just thinking that they reminded me of roses you read about in fairy tales."

Old Palmer shook his head. "Most o' these are modern hybrids, actually—but they're bred to look like the old antique roses. Gets the best from both worlds... see? They've got the big, full blooms an' proper perfume, an' they flower for months. Tough too. Proper shrub roses for growing in the garden... they can take what the weather throws at 'em."

"This colour is just gorgeous," said Caitlyn, indicating the creamy apricot bloom she had been sniffing.

The old gardener cracked a smile. "Aye, that's the 'Lady of Shalott'. She's one o' my favourites. A real beauty."

Then, to Caitlyn's surprise, he pulled a pair of pruning shears out of a rear pocket and cut off the bloom.

"Here ye go," He presented the rose to her.

"Oh! Thank you!" Caitlyn exclaimed. "I think that's the most beautiful flower anyone has ever given me."

"Get away with ye, now!" said the old gardener gruffly, but she could see from the twinkle in his eyes that he was pleased by her compliment.

"Are the rose gardens part of the official Manor tour?" she asked.

"No, they're not... but many o' the visitors come wandering down here by themselves anyway. An' the villagers are always welcome, of course. A couple of 'em are real busybodies—here every week, telling me how to prune an' what to use for blackspot... as if I don't know!" He growled. "That new tenant too. Always rabbiting on..."

Caitlyn's ears perked up. "From the refurbished cottages?"

"Aye, that woman with the bloody dog," he growled. "Little mutt running around loose an' digging up my flowerbeds... an' her! Walking around in them wellies... thinks she's a gardener, does she? Talking nonsense about azaleas! Even a green-behind-the-ears garden boy knows azaleas need acidic soil—"

"What about the young man? The English

teacher?" asked Caitlyn eagerly. "Do you see him?"

"Aye, he's a strange lad... mooches around... always asking if ye can grow black roses..." Old Palmer turned and pointed towards the far end of the rose garden, where it was backed by the woods that covered part of the estate. "There's a path there, through those trees, that leads to the cottages. Sort of a shortcut, ye see, instead o' going the long way from the main driveway. He likes to use that path an' cut through the rose gardens."

"Did you happen to see him two nights ago—the night of the Open-Air Cinema?"

The old gardener thought for a moment. "Two nights ago... hmm... Was out here doing a bit o' deadheading... Yes, now that ye mention it, I reckon I might have. Just when dusk was falling an' I was packing up."

"Was he in the rose garden?"

"No, I saw him on that path."

"What was he doing?"

The old gardener shrugged. "Couldn't really see... Could have been going, could have been coming... Wouldn't have seen him, actually, 'cept that I pricked my thumb an' the pain made me jump. Happened to look up an' see him."

"Wow, you must have really good eyesight," said Caitlyn, thinking of how hard it was to make out shapes at dusk, especially at a distance.

"Never need glasses," said Old Palmer proudly. "Not even for reading."

Caitlyn turned and scanned the area, noting that the woods stretched alongside the pathway and then flowed to the other side of the Manor, merging with the trees that surrounded the lawn where the cinema screen had been erected.

She thought back to yesterday afternoon, when Lionel Spelling had come into the chocolate shop. He'd insisted he hadn't gone to the Open-Air Cinema—that he'd stayed in his cottage all night—but could he have been lying? It would have been easy for him, especially in the black clothes that he usually wore, to slip into the woods from this side and make his way to the lawn without anyone seeing. It was just his bad luck that the old gardener happened to be tending his beloved roses and had such unusually good eyesight.

So had Lionel Spelling lied about where he'd been that night? Were the villagers right in their suspicions—was the young English teacher the murderer?

CHAPTER ELEVEN

After Palmer left her, Caitlyn wandered down to the path leading to the cottages and, out of idle curiosity, decided to follow it for a bit. She soon came to a section where there was a gap in the undergrowth next to the path and a track leading off into the woods. She felt a quickening of excitement. Lionel Spelling could have easily used this to enter the woods the night of the murder. She was just standing at the edge of the path, peering into the trees and trying to decide whether to explore, when she heard heavy footsteps behind her. She turned swiftly just as something large and furry shoved itself into her abdomen.

"Bran!" she said with a laugh as she put both hands on the English mastiff's head and gave him a gentle shove backwards. "You startled me."

The big dog wagged his tail, his baggy, jowly face creased into an amiable expression, then turned his body so that he leaned against her. She staggered slightly under his weight and patted his shoulder.

"Yes, okay, I love you too, Bran... but can you please not use me as a prop? You weigh a ton!"

He shoved his huge head into her abdomen again, making her double over. She realised that he wasn't just head-butting her for no reason—he was actually thrusting something at her: a soggy soft toy held in his mouth. She reached for it and, as she caught hold of one leg of the stuffed bunny, he pulled in the other direction.

"Oho! You want to play tug, do you?" chuckled Caitlyn. "All right, come on then!"

She tugged hard on the soft toy and the mastiff jerked his head in the other direction. Caitlyn felt herself being yanked forwards and had to brace her legs.

"Whoa! You're strong!" She laughed, putting both hands on the soft toy to get a better grip. She pulled again. The mastiff gave a playful growl and tugged in the opposite direction, dragging her in a circle. Caitlyn gave a squeal of laughter. Bran gave a muffled bark, wagging his tail, and then gave a great heave. Caitlyn yelped as she lost her grip on the toy and went reeling. She collided with something behind her and fell backwards, going down in a heap.

"*Uugh!*"

Caitlyn turned at the sound of the deep male voice and gasped in horror. Somehow, she had crashed into James Fitzroy, who had been standing behind her, and knocked him over backwards, landing on top of him. She was now sitting on his stomach. With a cry of mortification, Caitlyn scrambled to her feet, her face bright red.

"Oh God! I'm so sorry! I didn't see you—I mean—"

James stood up gingerly, coughing.

"Are you all right?" asked Caitlyn tentatively.

He coughed again. "Yes... yes... fine... Just winded me slightly."

Caitlyn squirmed in dismay. Why couldn't she ever meet James Fitzroy looking dainty, graceful, and elegant? Instead, she was either punching him in the face with a pillow or sitting on him with her big fat bum... It was no wonder James never saw her in a romantic light!

"I'm sorry..." she mumbled again.

"Not to worry, I've got plenty of ribs," said James with a teasing smile. "Losing a couple won't kill me."

Caitlyn relaxed and laughed.

"It looks like you and Bran are having a good time."

"Yeah, we were having a great game of tug-o-war."

James chuckled. "Oh, that's his favourite game. You have to be careful though. He's quite strong."

"Tell me about it!"

A familiar awkward silence descended over them. Caitlyn shifted from foot to foot, desperately trying to think of something to say. Why was it she felt relaxed and comfortable with every other man— even the handsome Antoine de Villiers—and yet when she met James Fitzroy, she always turned into a tongue-tied, blushing mess?

"Um… it's a beautiful morning, isn't it? Lovely sunshine…" mumbled Caitlyn. She couldn't believe that she was resorting to talking about the weather. Still, James was British… all Englishmen loved to talk about the weather, didn't they?

He glanced at the blue skies above them. "Yes, I'm hoping it'll hold for a few days, at least while my friends from London are here."

"Oh, yeah… I'd forgotten they were coming." Caitlyn licked her lips. "Um… are they old friends of yours?"

"Yes, mostly from college days. And a couple of chaps I used to work with when I was a foreign correspondent for the BBC."

"Do you miss your time there?"

"A bit. It was a very different lifestyle, continually moving to new locations, living out of a suitcase, sometimes travelling to very deprived or war-torn areas… It was certainly never dull!" He chuckled. "And I enjoyed meeting people and hearing their stories."

It's what makes him such a good landlord to his

tenants now, thought Caitlyn. She knew that while the Fitzroys were one of the last aristocratic families in England that belonged to the old "feudal" system—where they owned the village of Tillyhenge and all the estate around it—James was nothing like the traditional "lord of the manor". In fact, the villagers and farmers loved him for his ability to empathise with the "common man". He never mentioned his title and was quick to roll his sleeves up and join in with any of the work that needed doing.

"To be honest, it's been a bit of an adjustment, coming back to England and taking over the estate," admitted James. "I mean, I always knew in the back of my mind that I would be inheriting the title one day, but I suppose you tend to ignore these things until they're thrust upon you. It's been quite a steep learning curve in a way... and I know a few of the villagers and staff have been taken aback by some of the changes I've instigated..."

"I think you're doing a fantastic job," said Caitlyn. "I don't think there's any landlord that looks after his land and his people so well."

"Thanks," said James, looking embarrassed. Like most Englishmen, he was uncomfortable with compliments and hurriedly changed the subject. "It's tough for the farmers. Things are changing so much now; there is so much development in the countryside, with big corporations buying up land and turning them into modern housing—"

"Is that what Thane Blackmort wanted?" asked Caitlyn. She flushed slightly. "Sorry, I don't mean to pry, but I saw him at the Manor a few weeks ago and I've been wondering what he came for."

"Yes, he has been trying for several months to persuade me to sell part of the main estate, specifically the section that includes the ancient forest and the hill with the stone circle. I'm sure you've heard of Blackmort's reputation as a ruthless businessman—it's one reason he has become so wealthy and powerful—and I think he believed that I would cave in if the price was right."

Caitlyn drew a sharp breath. "You wouldn't ever sell, would you?"

"No, of course not. That is one of the oldest sections of the estate and has been in my family for centuries. In any case, it has great historical and cultural interest. I see it as my duty to preserve it."

"I'm so glad!" cried Caitlyn. "It would be awful if the stone circle and the forest were destroyed to make way for some ugly modern development."

James looked touched. "It's nice to meet someone who cares as passionately about the estate as I do," he said with a smile.

"Oh... um... well, anyone who has seen how beautiful it is would care..."

"And perhaps now that you've lived here for a while... it's beginning to feel like 'home'?" asked James gently.

"I... I don't know. I mean... I do have a home

back in the States. Barbara—my adoptive mother—she has a house in L.A. The lawyers are waiting for me to decide what I want to do..." She gave an uncertain laugh. "I know I should really be making plans but... well, so much has happened so quickly, I've just been taking each day as it comes... I haven't really thought about whether I'll stay in England..."

"I hope you'll decide to stay."

Caitlyn felt her heart give a little jump. "Well... I suppose I should wait to see what an English winter is like before I decide," she said, with an attempt at a light laugh. "California might suddenly look a lot more attractive after months of wind and rain."

James gave her a long look. "It would mean a lot to me if you stayed." He took a step towards her. "Caitlyn, I—"

He broke off suddenly, his gaze jerking to a point in the air beyond her. He frowned. "What the—!" He blinked incredulously. "Is that... Is that a pair of glasses?"

Caitlyn whirled around and her eyes bulged in horror. The Widow Mags's missing spectacles were hovering just above her head, like some kind of giant dragonfly. The next moment, they darted away in a blur of movement, pausing again to hover in the air above James's head.

"Wait... where's it gone?" James rubbed his eyes.

Caitlyn hoped fervently that he wouldn't look up. "Um... Where's what gone?" she asked brightly.

"Didn't you see it? It was there, in the air—above your head."

"See what?"

"A pair of flying..." James trailed off. He gave his head a sharp shake, then said with a sheepish laugh, "Never mind. I must be having hallucinations or something."

The spectacles darted sideways in another blur of movement. Caitlyn drew a sharp breath, thinking they might fly in front of James's face, but to her relief, they zoomed to the edge of the woods, hovered for a moment, and disappeared into the trees. Caitlyn sighed in relief.

Then they heard a faint call from the direction of the house and saw one of the garden boys in the distance, gesturing to James.

"Ah, this must be the overseas call I was expecting... Excuse me..." With another faintly puzzled look at the air above them, James gave her a distracted smile and headed back towards the Manor. Bran ambled after him, leaving Caitlyn alone at the edge of the rose garden. As soon as they were out of view, she turned and hurried to the track that led into the woods. *If I'm fast, I might still be able to catch up with the Widow Mags's spectacles and capture them.* She plunged into the undergrowth, following the track and jogging slowly through the trees, peering up into the canopy...

There they are!

Caitlyn put on a burst of speed and leapt into

the air, reaching out to grab the spectacles. Her fingers brushed the side of the frame but it slipped out of her reach.

"Rats!"

She raced after them as they zoomed through the trees, trying to grab them, jumping into the air—but the spectacles were quick and agile, evading her each time. Then the trees thinned and she ran into a small clearing in the woods. She faltered to a stop, staring at the structure in front of her, the runaway spectacles completely forgotten.

The ground in the clearing sloped upwards to form a small hill or a knoll, and sitting at the top was a crumbling stone tower that *really* looked like it had come straight out of a fairy tale. Caitlyn stared in wonder. She half expected to see Rapunzel lean out of the top and let down a long braid of golden hair!

As she got closer, however, she realised that wasn't actually as decrepit as it looked. In fact, it seemed almost as if it had been constructed to purposefully *resemble* a crumbling stone tower; but as she approached the base, she could see that it was a solid stone structure with a few "romantic" cosmetic touches. There was a large wooden door, studded with metalwork, cut into the side of the tower. She reached for the handle, wondering if it might be unlocked, and was pleased when it swung open with a loud creak of the hinges.

"Hello?"

Caitlyn stepped into the dusty interior. There wasn't a proper room inside—it was really nothing more than a giant stairwell, with a stone staircase spiralling upwards through the tower. She hesitated a moment, then started climbing up the steps. Small gaps had been cut into the stone walls at intervals, to let light in, but it was still very dim.

Forty-four... forty-five... forty-six... Caitlyn silently counted the steps as she climbed. *Sixty-two...sixty-three...* She paused, panting, and looked up. *How many more steps are there?*

When she came around the last curve of the staircase, she stopped and stared in dismay. The steps ended abruptly at another wooden door. This one was also studded with metalwork, but unlike the one below, it wouldn't budge when she turned the handle.

Caitlyn made a noise of frustration. She couldn't believe it! Had she climbed up all those steps for nothing? She tried the door again, jiggling the handle almost aggressively, but it was stuck fast. She sighed and turned away.

Then she froze. Was that the sound of footsteps?

She strained her ears. Yes, there was definitely someone moving around in the tower below. She realised uneasily that she was essentially trapped up here, with the steps leading to a "dead end" at the locked door and no way out but down the spiral staircase. She hesitated, then started quickly descending. Whatever or whoever it was, she decided she'd rather meet them head-on than remain skulking up here, wondering.

CHAPTER TWELVE

Caitlyn flew down the steps and was almost at the bottom when she met a man coming up. He stopped short at the sight of her, his face registering surprise.

"Oh! I beg your pardon—I didn't realise there was anyone else in here."

He had a clipped voice, with the words carefully enunciated, like someone who had gone to an etiquette school and been taught to speak "properly". He was also dressed in a very "proper" fashion, in a perfectly ironed, buttoned-up shirt and a conservative tie in a muted shade of navy. His hair was pale brown, cut short and neatly combed across his head, and his shoes were so highly polished that Caitlyn could almost see her own reflection.

He gave her a perfunctory smile and leaned backwards, making way for her to pass him on the narrow staircase.

"Ladies first," he said, sweeping a hand towards the bottom of the tower.

"Who are you?" asked Caitlyn, curiosity overcoming politeness.

"My name is Giles Mosley. I am the new butler at Huntingdon Manor."

"Oh." Caitlyn studied him. He was somewhere in his forties, she guessed, although it was hard to tell from his face, which had a curiously bland quality. He was the kind of person who would always fade into the background, blending easily without offering any information about his own personality.

She realised that she was staring and gave an embarrassed laugh. "Sorry... I've never met a real-life 'British butler' before."

"Ah... were you expecting something a bit more *Downton Abbey*?"

She grinned sheepishly. "I suppose."

"It is hard to shake off the traditional image—especially with the media fostering it—but modern butlers don't spend their lives polishing silver or standing in uniform by the front door, announcing visitors." He lifted his chin proudly. "We are a combination of concierge, estate manager, and personal assistant, helping our employers organise their lives and run their households. We organise the meals and entertainment, oversee the maintenance of house and gardens, supervise the other staff, attend to our employers' wardrobe..."

"Oh, so you're more like housekeepers now."

He bristled. "We are certainly more than housekeepers! Anyone can manage a house. The difference is, a properly trained British butler does it all with class and taste, grace and propriety," he said, drawing himself up to his full height and puffing his chest out.

His pompous manner made Caitlyn stifle a giggle. Keeping a straight face, she said, "Of course. I'm sorry—I didn't mean to offend."

He inclined his head in an almost regal fashion. "Not at all. It is a common misunderstanding. And I regret to say that even amongst the wealthy these days, there is a lack of appreciation for proper buttling. The *nouveau riche* are the worst." He gave a delicate shudder. "Those instant billionaires and others with 'new money' have absolutely no concept of how to conduct themselves. It can be quite a trial being in their employ. In fact, I just left a lucrative position in Dubai last month because I could not abide the lack of standards." He sniffed disdainfully.

"Lucky you found a new position so quickly," said Caitlyn.

He sniffed again. "A highly trained British butler such as myself is never short of offers." Then he softened and gave her a tight-lipped smile. "But yes, I was fortunate to find a position with Lord Fitzroy. It is increasingly rare now to be able to work for an 'old-money' family. One where they have had butlers for generations and don't need their servants to teach them how to conduct themselves with dignity." He gave her a look of mild curiosity and said, "And may I be so bold as to ask if madam is one of Lord Fitzroy's houseguests?"

His formal, old-fashioned words made Caitlyn want to laugh again. "Er... yes, I suppose you could say that. My cousin Pomona and I are staying at the Manor for a few days. I'm Caitlyn Le Fey."

He inclined his head deferentially. "It is a pleasure to meet you, madam. I presume you will be joining the party of guests arriving from London later today?"

Caitlyn nodded. "I was just having a walk before breakfast." She looked at him with curiosity. "By the way, what are *you* doing out here?"

"I was familiarising myself with the estate. Lord Fitzroy kindly gave me this morning off to 'settle in', as I have had little time to myself since arriving."

"Oh, yes—I remember James saying that you arrived only a day before the Open-Air Cinema Festival... It's been a bit of a rough start, hasn't it? Straight into a new household—and now there's a murder."

He stiffened slightly. "One is trained to deal with every eventuality."

"Were you out on the lawn when it happened?"

"No, I was in the Manor at the time, overseeing the post-movie refreshments. I was not made aware of the incident until I heard a commotion in the foyer. Naturally, as soon as I heard what had happened, I immediately notified the police."

"So you didn't see the victim?"

"I did see the paramedics transfer a body to the ambulance but I certainly didn't hover around with ghoulish curiosity!"

"Oh, no—I meant before the murder. Did you happen to see Pierre Rochat earlier in the day? I just wondered if you might have seen anything which might be a lead."

He raised his eyebrows slightly, obviously wondering why she was so interested, but his concern for propriety prevented him from questioning a guest's curiosity.

"Not that I recall," he said. "It was a very hectic day and I was busy supervising the staff and coordinating everything for the cinema event that evening, as well as familiarising myself with the normal household routines."

"Ah, right..." Caitlyn glanced at her watch. "Oh! Gosh, it's almost ten-thirty. I didn't realise how long I'd been out—I'd better get back. I haven't even had breakfast yet."

"If you wish to have an escort...?" he said, gesturing down the staircase.

"Oh, no, I'm fine walking back by myself. Don't worry about me. I'll see you later then!"

She hurried down the rest of the steps and made her way out of the tower, then retraced her route to the path that led to the rose gardens. When she arrived back at the Manor and walked into the Morning Room, she was surprised to see Inspector Walsh sitting with James, having a cup of coffee. They were deep in discussion but the inspector broke off as soon as Caitlyn stepped in.

"Oh! I'm sorry—" Caitlyn made as if to turn around and leave again but James called out:

"Caitlyn! Wait, don't go." He gestured to a seat at the table next to them. "Please—join us."

Inspector Walsh frowned. "Sir, I'm not sure that is wise—"

"Inspector, I trust Miss Le Fey implicitly. Anything you are happy to share with me can also be shared with her. She has my total confidence."

Caitlyn felt a warm flush of pleasure at James's words. They might not have been flowery compliments and yet somehow, coming from James, they meant even more.

The inspector hesitated, then resumed talking as Caitlyn took a seat opposite him.

"As I was saying, Lord Fitzroy, I have been talking to my colleagues at Scotland Yard and I've learned some interesting background information about the victim, Pierre Rochat. It seems that he has been on their radar for some time—they believe that he could have been a fence."

"A fence?" said James in surprise. "You mean... a receiver for stolen goods?"

"Jewellery in particular. Rochat's experience as

an antique jewellery dealer, and the fact that he travels extensively, provides him with the perfect set-up for the role. He could easily make contact with jewellery thieves and act as the middleman, selling their loot for them—for a nice commission, of course. We believe his murder may be linked to his criminal connections."

"But I don't understand—why should there be any connection?"

"Ah, well, we believe that Rochat may have been using Huntingdon Manor as a meeting place. In other words, the stolen jewellery was possibly being exchanged here—perhaps even on the night of the Open-Air Cinema. And as for a recent jewellery theft, well, there was a very high-profile raid of a boutique in London."

"Oh, yes, I read about that," said James. "Quite a daring robbery, I believe, of a jewellers in Mayfair, wasn't it?"

"Yes, Scotland Yard believe it was perpetrated by an infamous group of international jewellery thieves known as the 'Blue Magpies'. They favour dramatic, risky robberies, often in broad daylight—it's almost as if it is a game for them, a challenge to see if they can overcome the security measures and taunt the local authorities," said Inspector Walsh with a scowl. "Their last raid was of a jewellery store in a shopping mall in Dubai, only a few months ago, and now this recent robbery in London is also their work. Police were alerted and arrived on the scene just as they were making their getaway, and although the ringleader escaped with the loot, the police managed to apprehend the other gang members. But none of them are talking much."

"Was it a big robbery?" Caitlyn spoke up.

"In terms of items, no—there were only a dozen or so pieces of jewellery stolen—but amongst those pieces was a twelve-carat pink diamond worth several hundred thousand pounds."

James whistled. "I hope the boutique had good insurance."

"As it happens, the items didn't belong to the store. They were from a private collection which had been taken in for cleaning."

"And the thieves only stole jewellery from *that* collection?"

The inspector nodded.

"Meaning it probably wasn't just bad luck—they were targeting those items specifically. Maybe they knew the collection was going to be taken in to be cleaned and used it as an opportunity to steal the jewels," said Caitlyn.

The inspector nodded again. "Yes, that is what we believe. They must have had an informant— maybe someone in the staff of the private collector's household. And if I had to guess, I would say their main target was the pink diamond, as the other pieces were less valuable antique jewellery which had been in the family for generations: semi-precious stones like amethyst, topaz, bloodstone—"

"Bloodstone?" said Caitlyn, her ears perking up. "Like the ring that was stolen from the Manor a few months ago?"

The inspector looked at her in surprise. "Yes, that's right. Although there is no reason to suspect that the two pieces might be connected. Bloodstone is a popular gemstone used in vintage jewellery."

Caitlyn ignored his dismissive tone. The mystery of the missing bloodstone ring—which had never been recovered—had continued to bother her, despite the case now being closed. "Was the stolen bloodstone in a ring as well?" she asked.

"Hmm…" The inspector reached into his inner jacket pocket and took out a small tablet. He tapped it for a few moments, then turned it around and showed it to Caitlyn and James. The screen displayed a gallery of thumbnail pictures.

"This is a list of all the stolen items—no, this bloodstone wasn't in a ring. It was embedded in a brooch. Here it is."

He tapped one of the thumbnails, which enlarged to show an ornate antique silver brooch shaped like a key. The shaft was intricately carved and studded with tiny precious stones, all the way up to the wider "bow" end of the key, in which was embedded a large dull red stone. Caitlyn had seen a very similar stone before—or at least a picture of one.

"It looks like the bloodstone in the stolen Fitzroy ring!" she said excitedly.

Inspector Walsh made an impatient noise. "As I

said, it would be unwise to assume any connection between them. Bloodstones are a common semi-precious stone—"

"Not in that colour," Caitlyn pointed out. "Bloodstones are usually dark green with flecks of red. It's rare to find one that's primarily red. Don't you think it's odd that another one should turn up?"

The inspector waved a dismissive hand. "It could simply be coincidence."

Caitlyn looked at James. "Does this brooch look familiar to you? Is there any record of a bloodstone brooch in your family?"

"No," said James. "The only bloodstone jewellery I know of that belongs to the Fitzroys was the ring. However, that ring had been in my family for generations, and I don't know where it came from... so it *is* possible that it could have once been part of a set with a brooch—"

"In any case, this has no bearing on Pierre Rochat's murder," said Inspector Walsh, giving Caitlyn an impatient look. "While I appreciate that it would be nice to know if the stolen Fitzroy ring was a set with this stolen brooch, right now I have a murder investigation to conduct."

Caitlyn ducked her head. "Right. Sorry, I got sidetracked."

"So you think that Pierre Rochat's murder is connected to this gang of jewel thieves? The Blue Magpies?" James asked the inspector.

"Yes, after questioning gang members in custody, Scotland Yard deduced that the ringleader has fled into the countryside carrying the loot. In fact, I had a call this morning from my colleague, Inspector Devlin O'Connor of the Oxfordshire CID, who has received intel suggesting that the fugitives may be in this part of the Cotswolds. He requested that I keep an eye out for the ringleader, who may be posing as a tourist or temporary resident."

Or a new butler. Caitlyn was surprised by the thought that popped into her head. She didn't really think Giles Mosley could be a suspect in the murder... did she? Now that the thought had wriggled its way into her mind, it was hard to ignore. Was the new butler of Huntingdon Manor all that he appeared to be? Was it just coincidence that he should have arrived in Tillyhenge right before the cinema event, where Pierre Rochat had come to meet someone? Caitlyn thought back to the meeting in the tower this morning. Giles Mosley had seemed like a perfectly pleasant—if slightly pompous—man, but she knew that appearances could be deceptive. She glanced at the men and wondered if she should share her thoughts with James and the inspector... then decided against it. She had no proof, no basis for her suspicions—it was really just speculation— and besides, she was a bit embarrassed to suggest to James that his new butler might be a murderer.

She refocused on the present conversation and realised that James was asking Inspector Walsh about the scream on the night of the murder.

"...still haven't worked out who screamed that night. That person probably discovered the body. If you can just find him or her, you'd have a valuable witness."

"Yes, you're right, sir," Inspector Walsh agreed. "I've been neglecting that angle of the investigation. The villagers I interviewed were all adamant that they did not scream, which means someone else found the body—someone who hasn't come forward yet. I don't suppose you remember if the scream sounded male or female?"

James shook his head regretfully. "No. It all happened so fast. At first, I thought the scream had come from the movie—then I realised that it was coming from the back of the lawn, rather than the speakers. It was just a high-pitched cry of fear, which could have just as easily come from a man."

The inspector turned to Caitlyn. "Miss Le Fey?"

Caitlyn shook her head too. "Same here. I also thought it was the film at first... the woman in the film screamed just a few seconds before the real scream. So if I said 'female', I don't know if that's really what I heard or if it's just a subconscious association with the scream from the movie." She hesitated, then added, "Lionel Spelling, one of the new tenants, has a very high-pitched, feminine voice."

"Hmm..." said Inspector Walsh. "Yes, I am planning to speak to Mr Spelling again this afternoon."

"Have you asked him where he was on the night of the murder?"

"He claims he spent the night in his cottage—why?"

"Because I was speaking to Old Palmer—the head gardener—and he says he saw Spelling that night, on the path leading from the cottages."

"What was he doing?"

Caitlyn shrugged. "I don't know. I think it was too dark to see properly. But Old Palmer says it was definitely him."

"Can his eyesight be trusted?" asked the inspector. "It would have been just on twilight and things are notoriously difficult to see at that time."

"Oh yes," said James with a smile. "You probably couldn't find anyone with sharper eyesight than Old Palmer in the whole of the Cotswolds."

"In that case, I think I will go and speak to him now," said Inspector Walsh, rising from the table.

"What about Viktor?" said Caitlyn quickly. "You're releasing him today, right?"

The inspector hesitated, then admitted, "Yes, there is insufficient evidence to hold Mr Dracul in custody any longer. He will be released as soon as I get back to the station and give the order."

"That's great!" Caitlyn said in delight.

The inspector hesitated again, then cleared his throat and said, "Does Mr Dracul have family living in the area? We have attempted to find a relative to come and meet him when he is released today—however, we have been unsuccessful so far."

"Oh… well, I can come and pick him up," said Caitlyn. She caught the look of relief in the inspector's face and said, "Why? Is there a problem? Is Viktor all right?"

"No, no—no problem. Mr Dracul is fine. He seems to be suffering from a certain amount of confusion, but that is not unusual for a man of his advanced age."

"Confusion?"

"He appears to believe that he is a… er… vampire. He spent most of his interview yesterday telling me how he changes into a fruit bat."

"Oh." Caitlyn tried to hide her smile.

"He has also…" said Inspector Walsh with some asperity, "… eaten all the tins of fruit salad in the police canteen."

"Ah. Right," said Caitlyn, really struggling not to laugh now. "Well, I'm just going to have some breakfast while you're speaking to Old Palmer, then I'll follow you back to the station."

CHAPTER THIRTEEN

An hour later, Caitlyn found Viktor sitting in the police station canteen. He had already been released, and was greedily eating a can of pineapple chunks in sugar syrup. The lunch hour rush was obviously over and there was no one else in the cafeteria, aside from a canteen lady who watched Viktor suspiciously from behind the counter on the other side of the hatch.

The old vampire was slightly rumpled but otherwise seemed none the worse for wear after his experience.

"Ah, Caitlyn!" He beamed and waved his spoon. "This is the most marvellous stuff! You must try some."

"Oh, Viktor—I'm so glad they finally released you!"

He looked disgruntled. "Well, I did offer to remain and continue lending my assistance. I told the detective inspector that if he let me examine the body, I could tell him whether the puncture marks on the neck were made by a real vampire... but the ungrateful man did not seem remotely interested!"

Caitlyn smiled to herself. No, the pragmatic Inspector Walsh would not appreciate what seemed like a crazy old man asking to look for signs of the supernatural in a dead body!

"Well, it doesn't matter now," she said. "They've released you and that's the important thing. We can forget about it and let the police—"

"Forget about it? Certainly not!" cried Viktor. "We have to find the real murderer."

"But Viktor, it's nothing to do with you—"

"But of course it is to do with me! I cannot let the world think that vampires are bloodthirsty monsters—it is a matter of honour!" He wagged a bony finger at her. "Those ridiculous lies already being told, like vampires sleeping in coffins and being scorched by daylight—I quite like a spot of sun-bathing myself—those are bad enough, but this... this besmirches the good name of my kind! I must find the real murderer and put an end to these vicious rumours."

"But... what if the murderer *is* a vampire?"

"It is *most* unlikely to have been a vampire," Viktor blustered. "We vampires are part of an ancient order of noble guardians—we guide and protect—we do not stoop to murder."

"Yes, but what if there are vampires who don't follow that way of thinking? What if—"

"I shall prove to you that no vampire could have committed such a despicable act. I shall start an investigation of my own!" declared Viktor, raising a wrinkled fist and shaking it in the air. "I shall go into every house in Tillyhenge and plunder their secrets—"

"Uh... that might not be such a good idea," said Caitlyn hastily. She had visions of the old vampire blundering into people's homes, scaring everyone, and possibly getting himself attacked in the process. "You can't just go sneaking around in people's homes—"

"But they would never even know that I was there," said Viktor loftily. "My ability to glide through the shadows—what?" He broke off and glared at Caitlyn, who had guffawed involuntarily. She had seen Viktor's attempt to "glide through the shadows" once before and it had not ended well.

"N-nothing," said Caitlyn, still trying not to laugh. "I'm not sure... er... 'gliding' is as effective as you think."

"Nonsense! It is one of my great vampire talents—to move gracefully and invisibly with the cover of darkness... Very well, I shall demonstrate! I shall venture into the kitchen and retrieve a napkin from the shelf... and return... all with the canteen lady blissfully unaware of my presence."

He stood up grandly and wrapped his arms around himself, then twirled away—and promptly crashed into a nearby table.

"Er... I was just warming up..." muttered Viktor, straightening the table.

He cleared his throat, swept his arms dramatically around himself again, then spun towards the hatch that connected the canteen dining room with the kitchen. As he approached it, he spun faster and faster, until he was nothing more than a blur of grey—like a faint column of vapour, which slid through the opening of the hatch and into the kitchen beyond.

Caitlyn was impressed in spite of herself. Maybe she had misjudged Viktor. Maybe his vampire skills were more powerful than she realised—

There was a crash in the kitchen as something collided with the pots and pans stacked on a shelf next to the cooker. A minute later, the grey blur resolved itself into a balding old man in a dusty black suit, who tottered slightly, as if very dizzy, then toppled over sideways.

"Great..." Caitlyn sighed and ran over to the hatch.

She got there just in time to see Viktor on the floor, attempting to get to his feet again. Unfortunately, he rose up just as the canteen lady turned around to see what the commotion was about, and his head tangled in her skirts.

She gave a screech and yanked her skirt up,

revealing Viktor on his hands and knees, his few strands of grey hair in disarray around his bald head.

"Eeeeek!" she shrieked. "Trying to look up my skirts, are you? I'll teach you to sneak up on me, YOU DIRTY OLD MAN!" She grabbed a copper pot and began whacking Viktor on the head. "Take that! And that!"

Caitlyn groaned. She hurried into the kitchen and ran up to the canteen lady, managing to grab a beefy arm just as the latter was swinging the copper pot again. After a lot of placating and apologising, she managed to extricate Viktor and bundle him out of the canteen—and the police station. She didn't let go of him until she'd got him safely strapped into the front seat of her car.

"There was no need for such vicious behaviour," grumbled Viktor, rubbing a swelling on his forehead. "A slight miscalculation on my part, that was all."

Caitlyn sighed. "Look, Viktor—why don't you leave the 'investigation' to me? I'll do some asking around the village, okay? I promise I'll tell you anything I learn."

The old vampire protested indignantly and Caitlyn spent most of the drive back to Tillyhenge trying to mollify him. Finally, they came to a compromise where Viktor would accompany her but remain outside the buildings and let her do all the talking. As they arrived in the village green and parked the car, Caitlyn caught sight of the pub and had an idea: if Pierre Rochat really had come to Tillyhenge earlier in the day, he might have gone in for a drink. After all, the village was tiny and there were no other cafés or restaurants offering refreshments.

Leaving Viktor skulking around outside, she went into the pub and found Terry, the landlord, at his usual spot polishing glasses behind the bar. Caitlyn had a soft spot for the loquacious publican. Yes, he was a bit of an old woman and he could talk until the cows came home (and probably until after they were milked too) but he was one of the few villagers who had always been friendly and pleasant to her, despite her association with the Widow Mags, the "village witch".

The pub was Terry's pride and joy; his primary preoccupation in life seemed to be protecting it from drug dealers and maintaining its reputation as a respectable, law-abiding establishment. As such, he kept a fierce scrutiny on all patrons who entered, checking them with greater vigilance than a police sniffer dog. He was also always on the lookout for anything "dodgy" in the village, and constantly pestering the police hotline with reports of "suspicious activity".

He looked up now as Caitlyn approached the bar and said, shaking his head, "Bad business, this murder..."

"Were you there that night?" asked Caitlyn.

"No, but my missus was, told me all about it when she came back... Whole village is talking about it anyway—vampire murder, they say... Bollocks to that! No such thing as vampires... bound to be some local criminal... drugs, I shouldn't wonder... you never know where these drug dealers turn up... got to keep an eye out for them all the time... that's what I do... I run a clean establishment, me, and I'll have no drugs in my pub... that's what I say to my missus—"

"Uh... yes," cut in Caitlyn before he got on his favourite hobby horse. She knew that once Terry got started on the subject of keeping drug dealers out of his pub, it would be impossible to get him off the topic. "Um... so did you happen to see the victim, Pierre Rochat? I heard that he arrived in the village earlier in the day—I thought he might have come in here for a drink?"

The landlord gave her an approving look. "You're a smart lass. That's what the police asked me... Aye, he did... I served him myself... real nice gentleman, he was—not the type you'd think would get mixed up with criminals and such... but that just goes to show, doesn't it? Like I always say to my missus, you can never tell from the outside... these drug dealers look all respectable and—"

"Did you chat to him? Did he say what he was doing in Tillyhenge?"

"Wasn't too talkative, to tell you the truth... told me he was an antique jewellery dealer but wouldn't say much else..."

"Was he alone?" asked Caitlyn, wondering if Pierre Rochat had arranged to meet someone. "Did he speak to anyone?"

Terry shook his head. "Kept to himself. Sat at the corner of the bar, there, and had his drink."

"When did he come in?"

"Must have been 'bout three o'clock? Lunchtime rush was over and not teatime yet... normally a pretty quiet time in the pub... though if you get a coach of tourists arriving, bloody hell, things get busy... specially those Japanese groups—always wanting 'afternoon tea' and 'clotted cream'—I'm a blooming pub, not a teashop! My missus reckons we ought to start serving afternoon tea on them posh platters and charge twenty quid for the pleasure... twenty quid, I ask you! But she reckons the tourists would pay it and gladly—says she's been to a tearoom in Meadowford-on-Smythe that's doing rip-roaring business—The Little Stables, it's called—"

"Oh, I've been there!" said Caitlyn with a smile. "They've got the most delicious scones."

"Hmm..." Terry pondered this for a few seconds, then shrugged and said, "Suppose I could do with the extra business... have to be careful, mind, with all these tourists—you get all sorts... Dutch tourists, for instance... I hear there's a big drug scene in the Netherlands... and Columbia... and those Albanians are dodgy too—"

"So you didn't notice anything odd about Pierre Rochat?" asked Caitlyn, trying to steer the conversation back to the murder.

Terry shrugged. "Didn't know he was going to get himself murdered, did I? Would have been watching him more. Was more interested in that English teacher chap, to be honest."

"Lionel Spelling?" said Caitlyn, jerking upright. "He was here in the pub? At the same time?"

"Came in a few minutes after the Rochat fellow... dressed in those ridiculous clothes—"

"Did he speak to Pierre Rochat?" asked Caitlyn eagerly.

"No, no... sat at the other end of the bar and asked for his usual: elderberry wine... now, what kind of a drink is that, eh? Told the inspector, I did... there's something fishy going on with that young man—"

"Did he stay long?"

"Eh? No, left soon after the Rochat chap... didn't even finish his drink... not that I'm surprised... namby-pamby stuff... a pint of ale's what a real man should be drinking—"

"Er... Thanks, Terry—it's been great chatting to you!"

Caitlyn gave him a smile and hurried out of the pub, her thoughts churning. Was it just a coincidence that Lionel Spelling had come to the pub when Pierre Rochat was there? Or had the two men arranged to meet? Terry had said that the two men sat at opposite ends of the bar and hadn't talked to each other... but maybe that was done on purpose, to conceal their connection. They could have pre-arranged to meet there and then Rochat might have given Spelling a covert signal to follow him, right before he left the pub.

I've got to speak to Lionel Spelling again, thought Caitlyn.

Viktor pounced on her as soon as she stepped out of the pub. "You were an age in there," he said reproachfully.

"I've learned something interesting," said Caitlyn, and quickly repeated everything Terry had told her.

"Aha... excellent sleuthing!" said Viktor, rubbing his hands with glee. "We shall go to the workers' cottages now and I shall use vampire hypnosis to interrogate this Mr Spelling—"

"*We* are not going anywhere," said Caitlyn. "*I* am going to the cottages by myself and I'll *speak* to Lionel Spelling, not hypnotise him, but you're not coming with me." She saw Viktor's crestfallen expression and softened her tone. "Look, Viktor, it's better if I do it alone, okay? You'll just... complicate things."

The old vampire's shoulders drooped and he looked crushed. Caitlyn hesitated. Now she felt really bad. But she took a deep breath and hardened her heart. She knew that she was right— it was best if Viktor didn't accompany her.

"There's a new crop of fruit on the gooseberry

bush in the Widow Mags's garden," she said, giving him a persuasive smile. "Why don't you go back to *Bewitched by Chocolate* and wait for me there?"

Viktor nodded silently, turned and shuffled off. He looked so dejected that Caitlyn almost called him back. But she bit her tongue and resolutely turned in the opposite direction, heading for her car and setting off towards Huntingdon Manor.

CHAPTER FOURTEEN

When Caitlyn entered the Manor parklands, instead of following the driveway all the way up to the main entrance, she took the turn-off that led into the woods around the back of the house. This second driveway ended in a small farmyard which housed some of the Manor's farm vehicles and quad bikes. She parked the car and followed the winding pathway that led off from the farmyard, farther into the trees.

She had barely gone a few steps, however, when she heard a rustle in the bushes behind her, followed by a muffled *thump*. She turned swiftly but saw nothing behind her. After a moment, she started walking again, but within minutes the rustling started again, this time in the bushes next to her. There was a blur of motion in the air, a soft whooshing sound, and then another muffled *thump* as a tree trunk nearby shuddered from a sudden impact. A series of grumpy squeaks filled the air.

Caitlyn sighed. She knew that sound.

"Viktor? Are you following me?" she called, peering into the undergrowth.

Silence.

Caitlyn took a step deeper into the forest. "Viktor... I know you're there."

There was a moment's pause, then a fuzzy brown fruit bat crawled sulkily out from behind a bush.

"You're supposed to have gone back to wait for me at the chocolate shop!" cried Caitlyn.

The fruit bat made indignant squeaking noises and Caitlyn sighed again.

"All right, all right... you can stay but you can't come to the cottage with me—you have to wait here."

The little bat gave a grumbling squeak and flopped along the ground until it reached a tree trunk. Slowly, it began climbing the tree, using its bony little claws to hook into the bark as it hauled itself up. It looked so laborious that Caitlyn almost reached out to help but she resisted the urge, knowing that Viktor would probably be offended. She watched him affectionately as he made his way up into the lower branches. She would never have dared tell him to his face but Viktor was rather cute in his bat form, with the fuzzy brown fur covering his head and body, and his pointy little face and big black eyes... He looked more like a baby fox wearing a little black cape than a scary Halloween fiend.

She waited until he was hanging comfortably from a branch, his leathery wings wrapped around him like a blanket and his fuzzy little face peering at her upside down, before giving him a nod and saying, "I'll be back soon."

Then she turned and headed towards the cottages.

They were not joined together but they sat close to each other, side by side, each with a patch of garden in front. She didn't know the number of Lionel Spelling's cottage but it was easy enough to guess his from the outside. One cottage had a mountain of gardening paraphernalia piled by the front door—shiny new gumboots, gleaming spades and trowels, pretty gloves in a floral fabric, and a huge watering can, as well as an assortment of potted plants and flowers lining the path to the front door—whilst the front of the other cottage was bare, except for a few weeds. She guessed that the first cottage belonged to Gertrude Smith and, as she got closer, she saw a dog bowl on the front steps with the word "DOG" etched on the side.

Caitlyn walked past and went up the path to the second cottage. There was no bell so she rapped the old-fashioned knocker. No one answered. She waited a moment, then tried again. Still nothing. Frustrated, she stepped back from the door and leaned sideways to peer into the window, but the curtains were drawn and she could see nothing.

On an impulse, she walked back to the first cottage and knocked on the door there. After a few moments, Gertrude Smith flung open the door and stood on the threshold, eyeing her with suspicion. Rocco the terrier stood next to his mistress, wearing a similarly suspicious expression and growling deep in his throat.

"Whatever you're selling, I'm not interested!" Gertrude snapped and started to swing the door shut.

"No, wait!" said Caitlyn, catching hold of the door. She gave the woman a friendly smile. "We met at the Open-Air Cinema the other day—do you remember?"

The woman went pale and took a step back. "Yes, I remember," she said, her voice strained.

"Are you all right?" asked Caitlyn in concern, surprised at the change that had come over the woman. She put out a hand and touched her gently on the arm.

Gertrude Smith shook her off. "I'm fine. Just don't like to be reminded of that night, that's all." She gave a shudder.

"Oh, I'm sorry... I suppose it was rather upsetting—did you happen to see the body?"

The other woman gave a tight nod and swallowed convulsively, going even paler. Caitlyn was surprised. The last thing she had expected was for a practical, matronly type like Gertrude Smith to get squeamish about seeing a dead body. Still, you never knew how people responded to death, did you?

She cleared her throat and said, "I was actually looking for your neighbour—Mr Spelling. He doesn't seem to be in... have you seen him around today?"

"No."

Caitlyn tried again. "Do you see a lot of him? I mean, the two cottages being so close—"

"No," she snapped. "I don't go sticking my nose into other people's business." Then she relented and added, "I do see him sometimes, when I'm out in front, doing the weeding and such..."

She gestured to the gardening tools by the front door. Caitlyn followed the direction of her hand and took in the pile again. The equipment looked almost like a gleaming display at a garden centre.

"Did you see him on the night of the murder?"

Gertrude's expression tightened again. "No."

She really wasn't making it easy.

Caitlyn glanced around and tried again. "Um... so... are you here on holiday?"

"Yes. I fancied a quiet break in the countryside."

Caitlyn nodded at the gardening paraphernalia. "It looks like you've been busy."

"Yes, I love gardening," said the older woman smoothly. "Nothing like getting your hands in the soil and smelling the roses." The words sounded strangely clichéd and Gertrude seemed to realise this. She gave a gruff laugh and said, "I've been working in the corporate world for too long. Now I'm enjoying the slower pace and country pastimes, like going for walks... and doing my own baking..."

She waved a hand and Caitlyn realised that the other woman was clutching a rectangular cookie. The scent of cinnamon, nutmeg, and cloves wafted up and Caitlyn sniffed appreciatively.

"Mm... that smells delicious. Did you bake that?"

Reluctantly, the woman held out her hand. "Yes—would you like to try?"

Caitlyn took a piece and bit into it. It was a thin, crispy cookie, with a warm spicy flavour, unlike anything she'd tasted before. "Mmm... These are really good! What are they?"

"They're *speculaas*—traditional Dutch biscuits."

"Oh... are you from the Netherlands?"

"My family was originally from there, yes. And you? Your accent is quite unusual. I thought you were English at first—but at times you sound slightly American."

"Yes, I—"

A volley of barking from farther in the cottage interrupted their conversation.

Gertrude Smith spun in surprise. "What on earth—? Rocco?" She glanced around but the terrier was nowhere to be seen.

She hurried into the cottage and, after a second's hesitation, Caitlyn followed. They burst into the kitchen-dining room to find a scene of chaos. Rocco the terrier was running in circles around the table, bouncing up and down, and practically howling in frustration. At first, Caitlyn thought that he was barking at the large bowl of fruit in the centre of the table, but then she realised that there was something perched on top of the bowl.

A fuzzy brown fruit bat.

It was hugging one of the bananas and busily munching one end, an expression of contentment on its pointy little face.

Caitlyn groaned. What was Viktor doing in here?

"AAAaagh!" shrieked Gertrude Smith. "A bat! A nasty little bat!" She ran to a cupboard and returned a moment later brandishing a broom.

"No... wait..." protested Caitlyn, but she was thrust aside as the older woman charged towards the dining table, waving the broom.

Rocco barked furiously, his mistress's agitation making him even more manic. Caitlyn gasped as he leaped suddenly into the air and scrabbled to climb onto the table. He was too short to reach but he managed to get his front paws hooked on the edge and hung there, snarling and barking at the fruit bowl. The little bat jumped up, startled, and launched into the air just as Gertrude brought the broom down on the centre of the table.

WHACK!

The bowl of fruit exploded, apples and oranges rolling everywhere. Gertrude shrieked and swung the broom again, thrusting it wildly in several directions. Rocco raced in circles, barking excitedly, whilst the little bat gave ear-piercing squeaks as it flapped clumsily around the small room. It was absolute pandemonium.

"Get away! Get away, you filthy vermin!" yelled Gertrude, waving the broom.

The fruit bat crashed into the dresser, sending several plates and cups crashing to the ground, and hung precariously on one of the shelves.

WHACK!

The broom came down again, swatting the bat off the shelf and onto the floor. Rocco lunged, his teeth narrowly missing the little bat by inches as it jerked out of the way.

"No!" gasped Caitlyn, rushing forwards into the melee.

She could see that Viktor was cornered. Bats couldn't take off easily from the ground and he needed to climb up somewhere high enough to launch off. She had to distract the dog. But she didn't dare just grab Rocco—she had a feeling that the terrier could easily turn around and sink his sharp teeth into her hands. Maybe she could get his attention with a toy? She cast desperately around and spied a dog bed in the corner, with a stuffed toy rabbit in the rumpled blankets. She rushed to grab it but Gertrude caught her arm, yanking her backwards.

"What are you doing?" the other woman demanded. "Don't touch that! Rocco doesn't like anyone touching his toy!"

Oh, for heaven's sake... Caitlyn shot the woman an impatient look, then seized an apple that had fallen onto the floor instead. She lobbed it towards the terrier, who yelped with surprise as the apple bounced against him. The moment's distraction gave the fruit bat the chance to scuttle past the dog and climb onto one of the chairs.

"Arrrgh! Rocco had it and you let it escape!" cried Gertrude angrily. She rushed towards the bat again, swinging her broom.

The fruit bat took off, flying jerkily around the room, desperately searching for an escape route. Caitlyn rushed to the windows and flung them open, then stood back and shouted:

"Viktor! Over here!"

The little bat turned and swerved towards her, making a beeline for the open window and freedom. It swooped in a downward arc to avoid the swinging broom, but just as it was rising again the terrier lunged suddenly and sank his teeth into one of the bat's wings.

Caitlyn screamed. Rocco growled triumphantly as he clamped his jaws down hard and shook his head, flinging his prey from side to side. The fruit bat squeaked in alarm as it struggled to get free, flapping its other wing uselessly.

"NO! NO! LET HIM GO!" shouted Caitlyn, rushing forwards, not caring anymore about whether the dog might bite her.

She reached out to grab the terrier and just as

her hands touched his fur, something tingled at the tips of her fingers. There was a dazzle of bright light, a crackling noise, and then the barking stopped as if shut off by a switch.

The bat gave a faint squeak as it was suddenly released. It flapped clumsily up to the window ledge, climbed out, and disappeared.

There was silence in the cottage as Caitlyn stared in horror at what was in front of her. It was Rocco the terrier, with his eyes bulging and his mouth open and his teeth bared... in smooth milk chocolate.

"Rocco?" gasped Gertrude Smith, rushing over and crouching down next to the chocolate dog. "Oh my God, what have you done to my dog?"

"I... I..." Caitlyn stumbled backwards. She didn't know what to say. "I... I don't know..."

Turning blindly, she ran out of the cottage. Panic surged through her. What had she done? Could the spell be reversed? Could Rocco be turned back? She should have tried but she had no idea what she was doing and she was scared.

The Widow Mags, she thought suddenly. Her grandmother would know what to do. She was sure the old witch would be able to reverse the spell and fix everything.

Caitlyn started towards her car, then faltered to a stop as she remembered Viktor. She rushed around the cottage until she reached the outside of the kitchen windows and looked frantically around for him but she couldn't see a fruit bat—or a balding old man—anywhere. She shifted from foot to foot in an agony of indecision. She wanted to look for Viktor—what if he was injured and bleeding badly?—but she had no idea where to start searching. He could have been in the woods anywhere and it might take her hours to find him. And in the meantime... She bit her lip and glanced at Gertrude Smith's cottage. She couldn't leave Rocco like that... She had no idea how such spells worked, but maybe if he wasn't changed back within a certain window of time, he would "set" permanently as a chocolate dog.

Making up her mind, Caitlyn hurried towards her car. She would go and get help, then come back and search for Viktor as soon as she could.

CHAPTER FIFTEEN

Caitlyn burst into the kitchen at *Bewitched by Chocolate*, flushed and breathless. She was relieved to see the Widow Mags at her usual place beside the large wooden table, a chocolate-covered spatula in one hand and a bowl in the other. Bertha was sitting on the other side of the table, sipping a cup of tea, and both women looked up in surprise as she came barrelling through the back door.

"Quick! You've got to come... quickly... Rocco... I... I don't know what I did... the chocolate... can you change him back...?"

Bertha sprang up in concern. "I don't understand, dear—what are you talking about? Who's Rocco?"

Caitlyn waved her hands hysterically. "Gertrude... Gertrude Smith... he was going for

Viktor... I thought he would kill him... but I didn't mean—"

"Calm down, girl—we can't understand a word you're saying," said the Widow Mags. "Stop talking and take a deep breath."

Somehow, her grandmother's sharp reprimand did more to calm her than her aunt's gentle words. Caitlyn gulped and obeyed the Widow Mags. She took a shuddering breath, then let it out slowly, and felt her pulse steady. Taking another deep breath, she began to talk rapidly:

"I... I've put some kind of spell on Rocco—that's Gertrude Smith's terrier... she's one of the new tenants... I didn't do it on purpose, it just happened! He grabbed Viktor and had his wing in his mouth—Viktor had sneaked into the cottage in his bat form—I told him not to follow me!—and he was stealing from Gertrude Smith's fruit bowl but Rocco must have found him... and... and then there was total mayhem... and Gertrude was shrieking and I was terrified Rocco would hurt Viktor, so I reached out... and then I felt this... this thing at the tips of my fingers..."

She faltered to a stop as she saw that both women were staring at her, completely befuddled. Taking another deep breath, she tried again, this time telling the whole story from the beginning and forcing herself to speak slowly. When she finally finished, she looked desperately at the Widow Mags.

"You can fix it, can't you? You can undo the

spell?"

The old witch put down the spatula and walked over to the kitchen sink to wash her hands. "Yes, I should be able to undo it—but I'll have to see the dog first."

"What about Gertrude?" asked Caitlyn. "How are we going to explain it to her if she sees you turning a chocolate statue back into her dog?"

"Don't you worry about that," said Bertha, rising from her seat. "I'll make her a nice cuppa and she won't remember a thing."

"But—" Caitlyn started to protest.

"Stop fussing, child, and take us to the dog," said the Widow Mags.

Caitlyn gave up. She drove them at breakneck speed back to Gertrude Smith's cottage and they arrived to find the front door open. As they walked in, they nearly bumped into the woman herself hurrying out. She was carrying a suitcase and she scowled as she saw Caitlyn.

"You! Get out of here, you witch! You did something to my dog—"

"Now, now, there's no need to get excited," said Bertha, sounding like a nursery school teacher talking to a toddler having a tantrum. "It will all be sorted."

"What do you mean, 'it will all be sorted'?" the other woman retorted. "Have you seen my dog? He's been turned into bloody chocolate!"

"Oh, surely not?" said Bertha cheerfully. "You

must be imagining it."

"I am not imagining it!" spluttered Gertrude Smith. "If you don't believe me, I'll show you. Come inside!"

Bertha gave Caitlyn a wink as the other woman turned to lead them into the cottage. When they entered the dining room, Caitlyn winced. It looked like vandals had been through it with a sledgehammer. Broken china lay on the floor, a chair was overturned, fruit was scattered everywhere... and there, in the corner next to his bed, was Rocco the terrier—or rather, a chocolate replica of him—standing frozen in a pose of aggressive attack.

"There! You see?" Gertrude pointed an accusing finger. "He's... he's... he's been turned to chocolate! But he can't be, right? I mean, how can a dog turn into chocolate? Oh God, first Rochat and the vampire... now this... am I going mad?"

"There, there..." said Bertha, catching hold of the other woman's arm and steering her towards a chair at the dining table. "It's almost four o'clock. Let's have a nice cup of tea, shall we?"

Gertrude shook her arm off roughly. "I don't want a bloody cup of tea! I want an explanation! What's she done to my dog?" She glared at Caitlyn, who shrank back. "He was such a brilliant guard dog too. Now what am I going to do?"

Caitlyn had been feeling a bit sorry for the woman but now her sympathy vanished. Gertrude

Smith's distress didn't seem to be for the dog himself but rather for her own selfish needs. Bertha ignored her and went into the kitchen, returning a few minutes later with a steaming mug, which she thrust at Gertrude.

"Here, drink this; I promise you'll feel better."

"There's nothing wrong with *me*," Gertrude snapped. "It's my dog! It's—"

"Just drink up," said Bertha in a firmer voice.

To Caitlyn's surprise, the other woman took the mug. Maybe there was magic involved... or maybe it was simply Bertha's manner—she reminded Caitlyn of a motherly but brisk, no-nonsense nanny from childhood, whom you obeyed without question. Gertrude Smith obediently began to drink the hot tea. A moment later, she set the half-finished mug down with a sigh.

"I need to finish packing..." she mumbled, making a motion to rise. "I need to go—"

Bertha pushed her gently back into the chair. "There's no rush. Why don't you just rest for a moment, hmm? I'm sure you must feel tired after all the excitement earlier."

"I do feel exhausted now that you mention it..." Gertrude admitted, sinking back into the chair. She gave a great yawn... then another, and leaned her elbows on the table. "...almost feel like having a nap..."

"Well, why don't you?" asked Bertha pleasantly.

"...but the packing..." Gertrude mumbled, as her

head drooped lower and lower. "...need to get out... place is getting too hot..." She flopped onto the table with her head on her arms and, the next moment, she was fast asleep.

"Wow," said Caitlyn. "What was in that tea?"

"Oh, nothing that will harm her," said Bertha with a smile. She patted her pocket. "Lucky I had a couple of sachets of special herbal tea with me... she'll just have a little sleep and wake up refreshed and relaxed—and none the wiser."

The Widow Mags walked over to the chocolate terrier and picked it up. Caitlyn watched as the old witch examined the dog.

"Can you restore him?" she asked anxiously.

"Hmm... it would have been easier if I knew what spell you used. As it is, I will have to guess..." She rolled up her sleeves, held out her hands over the chocolate terrier, and chanted:

"Unknown spell, I hereby quell,
Unknown magic, I render static,
Unknown charm, I now disarm,
Undo thyself, Leave no harm!"

There was a humming sound and the chocolate dog glowed suddenly, then—like snow melting—the chocolate peeled away from the tops of his ears, down his muzzle, along his back, and to the tip of his tail. A moment later, a snarling terrier stood in front of them.

"YAP-YAP-YAP-YAP-YAP!"

"Huh?" Gertrude Smith started awake and looked around in bewilderment. Then her eyes fell on the terrier. "Rocco!" she cried. She sprang up from the chair and looked at them accusingly. "You've changed him back!"

"I'm sorry? I'm afraid I don't know what you mean," said Bertha.

Gertrude pointed at the dog. "My dog had been turned to chocolate."

"Chocolate?" Bertha gave a trill of laughter. "What nonsense! How can a dog be turned into chocolate?"

"He was! He was completely stiff, like a chocolate statue—"

"I think you must have had a dream," said Bertha. "It's quite common when you have a nap in the heat—"

"I didn't have a nap!" snapped Gertrude. "And I didn't dream it! I'm telling you, I saw it with my own eyes. And anyway, what are you doing in my house?"

"Oh, we were just walking past and happened to see your front door open. We were worried—you know, what with the murder that's happened recently and you being a woman living on your own—so we came in to check on you," said Bertha. "You were lying there, with your head on the table, fast asleep."

"I... I was?" Gertrude turned to look at the table,

for the first time uncertain. "But I could have sworn..."

"Well, not to worry. We can see that you're fine so we'll leave you now," said Bertha brightly, turning to hustle Caitlyn and the Widow Mags out of the kitchen. "Enjoy the rest of your afternoon!"

They left Gertrude Smith still staring at her dog in bewilderment and hurried out of the cottage.

"Wow," whispered Caitlyn, eyeing her aunt with admiration. "I thought Pomona was a brilliant liar but you'd give her a run for her money!"

Bertha laughed modestly. "I try not to make a habit of it."

As they walked away from Gertrude Smith's cottage and headed for her car, Caitlyn was surprised to realise that it was already late afternoon. Somehow the day had run away from her. She'd had such a late breakfast that she hadn't felt hungry at lunchtime, but now she felt her stomach rumble.

"Some food and a cup of hot chocolate for you, young lady," said Bertha, eyeing her shrewdly. "Come on—I'll make you something when we get back to the chocolate shop. Mum's just made a fresh batch of chocolate fudge brownies."

"Wait! What about Viktor?" cried Caitlyn, suddenly remembering. "He's hurt—we've got to find him!"

"I thought you said he escaped through the window?" said Bertha.

"Yes, but not until after Rocco took a chunk out of his wing."

"Was he bleeding? Could he still fly?"

"I didn't see any blood," Caitlyn admitted. "And yes, he was flying—sort of. He was a bit lopsided but he did manage to get up through the window and take off. I searched a bit around the cottage before I came to get you but I couldn't see him anywhere."

"That means he was well enough to fly into the woods," said Bertha.

"That old bat's been in worse scrapes than this," said the Widow Mags. "Don't worry—he'll be fine."

"But—"

"Vampires have extraordinary healing abilities," Bertha explained. "It is one of the reasons they live so long. And bat wing membrane is one of the fastest healing tissues, even in nature. Don't worry—I'm sure Viktor can take care of himself. If he hasn't turned up by tomorrow, then you can worry."

Caitlyn cast a last look into the woods, then sighed. "All right. But if I don't hear from him by tomorrow morning, I'm going to come back here and search the woods for him."

CHAPTER SIXTEEN

When Caitlyn returned to the Manor that evening, she wondered where Pomona was. She hadn't seen her cousin all day and was bursting to tell her everything that had happened.

The new butler greeted her at the door.

"Miss Sinclair?" he replied when she asked about Pomona. "I believe she has gone up to her room to change for dinner. Lord Fitzroy's London guests arrived this afternoon and there is to be a formal meal in the Dining Room."

Caitlyn realised guiltily that she had forgotten about the new guests and dinner that night. As she started climbing up the sweeping staircase, she worried if she had packed anything she could wear to a formal dinner. When she reached the door of the room she shared with Pomona, however, her steps faltered. The memory of their fight yesterday came back to her. Would Pomona still give her the silent treatment?

For a moment, she felt a surge of irritation at her cousin again, then she paused and admitted that perhaps they had both been at fault. Now that she was calmer, she knew that Pomona had meant well and had spoken out of genuine concern, not jealousy. It had been very flattering, getting all that attention, and her ego had been bruised by her cousin's suggestion that Antoine de Villiers hadn't been sincere. But it wasn't worth fighting with her best friend. She would swallow her pride, apologise to Pomona, and make up.

Caitlyn turned the door handle and stepped into the bedroom. Her cousin was standing, looking out of the window, but she turned swiftly at the sound of the door.

Caitlyn gave her a tentative smile. "Hi..."

"Hi..." Pomona said in return.

There was a strained silence for a moment, then both girls started speaking at once.

"Pomona, I'm sorry about yesterday—"

"Oh Caitlyn! I was just gonna come and look for you! I wanted to apologise—"

Both of them stopped and stared at each other, then gave an embarrassed laugh.

"You were coming to apologise?" said Caitlyn.

"Just this one time," said Pomona quickly. "Don't think it's gonna become a regular occurrence."

Caitlyn grinned. She was incredibly touched. "Thanks, Pomie. And... and I'm sorry for what I said yesterday—I know you're just watching out for me... I don't want us fighting just because of some guy."

"No," Pomona agreed. "No guy's ever gonna come between us." She ran over and flung her arms around Caitlyn, squeezing her in a tight hug. "Oh Caitlyn! I've missed you!"

"I've missed you too," said Caitlyn, hugging her back. Then she let go, saying excitedly, "I've got so much to tell you!"

Quickly she filled Pomona in on what she'd been up to. "I just hope Viktor's okay," she finished at last with a sigh.

"He'll be all right," said Pomona. "He's a tough old cookie." She flopped down on her bed and leaned back on her hands, looking up at Caitlyn with a smug smile. "You're not the only one who's been busy sleuthing today, you know."

"What do you mean?"

"I got chatting to one of the police sergeants hanging around the crime scene... very young... very cute..." Pomona grinned.

Caitlyn looked at her cousin in disbelief. "You seduced one of Inspector Walsh's men?"

"Who said anything about seduction? I just gave him a smile as I was walking past..."

Caitlyn shook her head wryly. She knew all about Pomona's famous smiles. One look and most men were goners. Especially young, impressionable men.

"So what did he tell you?"

"He said he loved my voice… and my eyes were bluer than the Mediterranean Sea… and if I was free next weekend, he knew this great place in Cheltenham—"

"Pomie!"

"All right, all right," said her cousin, grinning. "He told me the results of the autopsy."

"*Really?*" Caitlyn looked at the other girl with admiration. "What did the report say?"

"Ah… well, this is the interesting bit…" Pomona paused dramatically. "Pierre Rochat's body had been drained of blood!"

"What?"

"Well, not totally drained," Pomona admitted. "Just, like, one third—but apparently one third is enough to kill you 'cos your heartbeat starts going irregular and you get cardiac arrest and organ failure… blah-blah… I have to admit, I wasn't really listening properly after that—I was too busy admiring his ginger eyelashes. Yeah, seriously, *ginger.*"

"There's nothing wrong with red hair," said Caitlyn, touching her own auburn curls.

"On a woman," said Pomona. "On a guy, it's totally different. But I have to admit, he was kinda cute, even with the ginger hair. And there's just something so sexy about the British accent, even when it's not 'posh' like James's—"

"Pomie...!" Caitlyn said in exasperation. "What else did the autopsy report say?"

"Huh? Oh... oh yeah... so, the cause of death was shock from blood loss."

"What about the puncture marks on his neck? Were they made by fangs?"

"They could be!" said Pomona. "The pathologist wasn't sure. The report said *maybe* it was some kind of weapon shaped like fangs... but I think the police are just trying to find a non-supernatural explanation, 'cos they don't wanna admit that it could be a vampire!"

"Inspector Walsh thinks it was *made* to look like a vampire murder, by someone using fangs from an animal—you know, like the skull of a wolf or tiger."

"Where would you get that?" demanded Pomona. "And anyway, even if they did, wouldn't there be blood everywhere?"

"What do you mean?"

"Well, this cute sergeant told me that the only way to lose that amount of blood that quickly was if you punctured the carotid artery in the side of the neck. But arteries are, like, under really high pressure—so if the killer had done that, wouldn't there have been blood spraying everywhere? You were on the scene—did you see a lot of blood?"

"No," Caitlyn admitted. "I didn't see any, as a matter of fact. Just Rochat's body... and the puncture holes in his neck."

"You see? If it was a vampire, he would have

sucked the blood up and that's why you didn't see a drop anywhere."

That was exactly what Beth Jenkins had said. Caitlyn frowned, not wanting to accept that the village gossips could be right.

"Well, maybe... maybe the murderer used some kind of machine," she suggested. "You know, like undertakers or morticians use... don't they suck the blood out of bodies and replace it with embalming fluid or something?"

"Oh, *puh-lease!*" said Pomona, rolling her eyes in an exaggerated fashion. "You think the murderer managed to do all that in the dark, in the middle of the forest?"

Caitlyn said nothing. Her cousin had a point. Still, she was reluctant to accept that the murderer could have been a vampire—maybe because the idea was so creepy. Somehow, thinking that Pierre Rochat was killed by a fugitive jewellery thief was a lot easier to swallow.

"I still think for once Inspector Walsh is right and there is no paranormal angle in this case," she said stubbornly. "I think Pierre Rochat was murdered because of his role as a fence for jewellery thieves. Maybe there was some double dealing... or an exchange that went wrong..."

"So what are you saying—that the murderer was one of the thieves?" Pomona asked.

"Yes, the ringleader. Inspector Walsh thinks he's hiding out here in the Cotswolds with the loot—

maybe even right here in Tillyhenge—and that's the real reason Rochat came to the village. So if the murderer is the ringleader, then it's likely to be someone who was a recent arrival... like Lionel Spelling."

"That Goth guy?"

"There does seem to be a lot of stuff pointing towards him. He lied about where he was on the night of the murder, he had an easy route through the woods to reach the cinema lawn unseen, he was in the pub at the same time as Pierre Rochat—and left straight after—and... well, he's just a bit of a weirdo."

"Being a Goth doesn't make you a criminal," protested Pomona. "It's just a fashion and lifestyle statement."

"I guess... but it does mean that he's more familiar with vampire lore and stuff like that, doesn't it?"

"Maybe. But why would he wanna kill Pierre Rochat? I mean, he's, like, a language school teacher, not some international jewel thief!"

"Maybe he's both," said Caitlyn. "The teacher thing could be a front for his criminal activities."

Pomona rolled her eyes. "If we're talking about fronts, I can think of a better job for that: someone who lives with the rich, knows all about their expensive jewellery, travels around a lot... a butler."

"A butler?"

"Yeah." Pomona glanced at their closed bedroom

door and lowered her voice. "That guy—Giles Mosley—the new butler here at the Manor."

"Well, I have to admit, I did think of him myself," said Caitlyn. "I mean, Mosley told me that his last job was in Dubai... and that's where the last robbery by the Blue Magpies took place. I suppose it could just be coincidence but..."

"Too many coincidences." Pomona leaned forwards. "And don't you think it's a bit weird that he was out in that tower? I mean, it's not the kind of place you'd expect a prim and proper butler to be in."

"I suppose... although he could have just been exploring the estate, like he said. He only arrived a few days ago and it's natural to be curious about the place you're going to live in. Besides, Pomie, if you'd seen this tower, you'd see why anyone would be curious about it. It looked like something straight out of a fairy tale."

"Why is it there, in the middle of the woods?"

"I don't know—I suppose I can ask James tonight."

Pomona straightened her sheets and said in a carefully casual voice, "You know, there *is* another person who could be a suspect as well: he came to Tillyhenge recently, he's stinking rich, and he moves in all the right circles so he'd know about expensive jewellery... plus he was at the Open-Air Cinema and he met Pierre Rochat..."

"Don't tell me you're thinking of Antoine de

Villiers!" groaned Caitlyn.

"Aww, come on! You can't rule someone out just 'cos he's hot!"

"You do all the time," Caitlyn muttered. "You did it with that Irish gardener."

"That was different." Pomona waved a dismissive hand. "Seriously, I think we've got to consider—"

"Why would Antoine want to murder Pierre Rochat? He didn't even know the man! You're not suggesting that he's a jewellery thief, are you?"

"Why not?" retorted Pomona. "To be honest, I can see him as a jewellery gang ringleader much more easily than Lionel Spelling or Giles Mosley!"

"It's not Antoine—he owns a *chateau*, for heaven's sake! Why on earth would he need to steal jewellery?"

"For kicks? He looks like the kind of man who enjoys taking risks. Maybe he's bored—lots of rich people are bored and, like, looking for new thrills. You know, like that guy in *The Thomas Crowne Affair.*"

"That was a movie!"

"Doesn't mean it couldn't have been based on real life. You've seen the celebrities in Hollywood... People who've got everything are always searching for the next thing to make their life interesting."

"You're getting very deep all of a sudden," said Caitlyn sarcastically. "I'm telling you—it's not Antoine. I know. He's a gentleman and—"

Pomona burst out laughing. "Honey, Antoine de

Villiers is a lotta things but a gentleman he is not. Trust me, *I* know."

"Let's not fight about him again."

Pomona sighed. "Okay. But at least... keep an open mind about him?"

"Fine," said Caitlyn grudgingly. "In fact, when I see him tonight, I'll try to ask him about Rochat."

"Speaking of tonight, what are you gonna wear?"

"Tonight?" Caitlyn looked at her blankly, confused by the sudden change of topic.

"Yeah, the formal dinner! You can't show up in your usual jeans."

"I wasn't going to," said Caitlyn defensively. "I was going to wear... uh..."

"Don't worry, coz, I've got it sorted," said Pomona with a grin. "I went down to Angela's boutique today and picked up something for you."

"You didn't let her do any alterations on it, did you?" asked Caitlyn with a dark look.

Angela Skinner was a resident of Tillyhenge who made no secret of her contempt for the Widow Mags and her enchanted chocolate shop—nor her jealousy of Caitlyn. After unsuccessfully trying to bully the Widow Mags in her own store (and ending up with chocolate warts in the process), the young woman had then tried to play a mean trick on Caitlyn by stitching up a dress so that it was too tight to wear, right before the all-important Fitzroys' Summer Garden Party. Luckily, a bit of magic—and "chocolate spandex"—had come to the rescue, but

Caitlyn had learned not to trust Angela after that. Still, she had to admit that the woman had exquisite taste and her dress boutique in the village stocked pieces that wouldn't have looked out of place on a Paris catwalk.

"What did you get? Can I see?" she asked excitedly.

"Only if you let me do a makeover," said Pomona.

Caitlyn gave a resigned laugh. Her cousin never gave up! Pomona had been begging to give her a makeover ever since they were teenagers.

"Oh, all right..." said Caitlyn, capitulating at last. "But nothing too major! I don't want cat eyes or bee-stung lips or whatever other weird trend is going around the fashion world right now."

"You won't even know you have make-up on," Pomona promised. "You'll look just like yourself—but, like, ten times prettier!"

CHAPTER SEVENTEEN

Caitlyn followed Pomona down the staircase that evening, nervous and excited. She had barely recognised herself when she looked in the mirror before leaving their bedroom. Her red tresses had been twisted up into an elegant knot, with a few loose tendrils framing her face, and her face had been expertly made up to highlight her hazel eyes, turning them a luminous green, fringed by thick black lashes.

The dress that Pomona had chosen was in a simple but sophisticated style—a deep indigo purple wraparound sheath that brought out the creamy tones of her pale skin and made her red hair seem even more vibrant. Caitlyn had been horrified at first at how closely the dress hugged her body—she normally chose baggy styles to try and disguise her big hips—but then she realised that with the right cut and fabric, a dress could actually flatter her curves, giving her a classic hourglass figure. *Maybe Pomona was right all along*, she thought. You had to work *with* your curves, not try to hide them.

Now, she descended the sweeping staircase feeling more beautiful than she had ever done in her life. Her heart pounded as she entered the Drawing Room, where everyone was meeting for drinks before dinner. Would James notice the difference in her? Would he like it?

Giles Mosley was waiting to receive them with a tray of champagne flutes. The butler was in full uniform—black morning coat with tails, grey waistcoat, starched white shirt with a black tie, and even white gloves—and looked slightly comical, although he took himself so seriously that Caitlyn didn't dare even crack a smile. She thought again of Pomona's suspicions about the Manor's new staff member. It was true that his uniform would've made a very effective disguise, and his butler training might have given him the perfect organisational and project management skills to pull off a heist! And yet somehow she just couldn't see Giles Mosley as a criminal ringleader. He seemed so pompous and "proper" that he would've probably considered jewellery robbery beneath him! Well, unless he was stealing the Crown Jewels, perhaps—jewels worn by the Royal Family might just be worth sullying his hands for...

The thought made Caitlyn smile and she hurriedly turned away so that Mosley couldn't see. She raised her champagne glass and sipped the sparkling, golden liquid as she surveyed the other guests. She was glad that she had listened to Pomona's advice. Everyone was stylishly dressed, with the women in particular having gone to great effort for the evening, and for once, Caitlyn didn't feel like the ugly duckling in a group of swans. In fact, she flushed with pleasure as several women eyed her with admiration and complimented her appearance.

Then she looked up and her eyes met James's on the other side of the room. He was looking at her like he had never seen her before and Caitlyn's heart skipped a beat. Slowly, he began to weave his way towards her and Caitlyn felt her pulse beat faster and faster. Before he reached her, however, another man stepped in front of him.

"You are a vision of loveliness, *mademoiselle*," Antoine de Villiers said, raising her free hand to his mouth.

"Th... thanks," said Caitlyn. She pulled her hand away, embarrassed.

"I hope you are sitting next to me this evening?"

"I don't know," said Caitlyn honestly.

Antoine gave her a teasing smile. "Ah... but I hope you *want* to?"

"Er... well..." Caitlyn fumbled. She didn't want to be rude. "Um... of course."

"Caitlyn is sitting next to me," said a deep voice behind them.

They turned to see James Fitzroy watching with a slight frown. He stepped forwards and his grey eyes warmed as he looked at Caitlyn.

"You look beautiful," he said quietly.

Caitlyn flushed with pleasure. "Thank you."

It was a novel sensation, having the admiration of two handsome men, and she felt a bit like she was floating on a cloud—although perhaps that was also the effect of the champagne on her empty stomach. In fact, by the time dinner was announced, she had drained the whole flute and felt quite light-headed. She wasn't the only one. All the guests seemed to be in a jovial mood and the atmosphere was merry as the group drifted into the grand Dining Room for the meal. The long mahogany table was laid with gleaming silver and beautiful Wedgewood crockery, and the sparkling wine glasses seemed to catch the light from the huge chandelier. A small place card inscribed with each guest's name in beautiful calligraphy was placed in front of each seat. The Manor's maids were hurrying to and fro, arranging plates of food, whilst Giles Mosley carefully uncorked a bottle of wine at the buffet table nearby.

As everyone was about to take their seats, a soft knock sounded behind them. Caitlyn turned to see a pretty young woman with honey-blonde hair and an English-rose complexion hesitating in the Dining

Room doorway. It was Amy Matthews, whose late husband, Huntingdon Manor's gamekeeper, had been murdered a few months ago. Caitlyn knew that James had been very kind to Amy following his death, letting her remain in her cottage rent-free and even offering her a job as a personal assistant, when Amy had struggled to find work in the local area.

Of course, there were whispers in the village that Lord Fitzroy's solicitude stemmed from more than just his usual concern for his tenants. Caitlyn had heard the rumours and she wasn't surprised. James and Amy were of a similar age and made such a handsome couple—it was no wonder that tongues had been wagging. Now as she saw Amy standing gracefully in the doorway, slim and pretty in a simple navy dress, Caitlyn thought with a pang that Amy would make a lovely Lady Fitzroy.

"Sorry to bother you, James," said Amy, holding up a piece of paper. "I just wondered if you wanted to check this so I can make any changes before I leave... although I'm happy to come in early tomorrow morning, so you can have it before your meeting—"

"Good God, Amy, I thought you'd left ages ago," said James. "Don't feel that you have to slave in the office until late, you know. That document could have waited until the morning."

Amy laughed. "I know—but I like to get the work done and make sure you've got everything you need."

"You're an exemplary PA—I don't know what I'd do without you," said James with a smile.

Amy blushed and began turning away, but James put out a hand to stop her.

"Wait, Amy, don't run off—why don't you join us for dinner?"

"Oh no, I wouldn't want to impose—"

"Don't be silly, you're not imposing. I'm sure everyone would love to have you."

There was a murmur of assent around the table and everyone nodded and smiled at Amy.

The young woman looked at the guests, then down at herself. "I'm not really dressed properly—"

"Nonsense, you look lovely," said James gallantly.

Caitlyn felt a prickle in her breast and was ashamed to realise that it was jealousy.

"Well... thank you," said Amy with a shy smile, approaching the table.

"*Voilà, mademoiselle*, you can sit here—next to James," said Antoine de Villiers, deftly removing a place card from the seat beside James and moving it to the empty seat next to his chair.

Caitlyn realised with dismay that the card that he had moved was printed with her name. She was now seated next to the Frenchman and Amy would be taking her place next to James Fitzroy. She glanced at James, wondering if he would say something, but he was silent. Maybe he didn't want to embarrass Amy by making a scene. *Or maybe he'd prefer to sit next to her*, thought Caitlyn, with a hollow feeling in the pit of her stomach.

Everyone sat down and there was much *oohing* and *aahing* over the dishes on display. Mrs Pruitt, the Manor's cook—or Catering Manager, as she was now called—had outdone herself. She had been frustrated ever since James took over the title and rejected the elaborate three-course dinners that his father used to expect every night, instead opting for simple meals on trays in his study. So with the excuse of the London guests, she had taken the opportunity to put on a veritable feast. There was a refreshing lobster salad to start, with crisp sliced apples, watercress, and candied walnuts, followed by a creamy soup of minted peas; next came *pan-fried sea trout with Scottish mussels*, and succulent *corn-fed chicken breast with lemon verbena seasoning;* and finally, the star of the show: *traditional roast beef with Yorkshire pudding, slow-roasted carrots, creamed Savoy cabbage, and duck-fat-roasted potatoes, together with gravy and horseradish sauce.*

Conversation flowed easily as everyone began to eat, with James's friends sharing amusing anecdotes about life in the big city. Despite having only met them earlier that afternoon, Pomona was obviously at home with the young crowd, laughing and joking along with them. Caitlyn's natural shyness meant that she found it harder to strike up conversation with strangers and so she was glad, in a way, to be sitting next to Antoine. The Frenchman seemed only to have eyes for her, despite several of the female guests sending flirtatious glances his way, and once again, Caitlyn was flattered in spite of herself.

She was also very aware of James at the other end of the table, with Amy sitting next to him. The sight of them talking and laughing together brought a stab of jealousy again, and when James glanced up and caught her eye, she deliberately turned to Antoine de Villiers and gave him a dazzling smile.

She was being petty, she knew, but she couldn't seem to help herself. There was an uncomfortable churning in the pit of her stomach and Caitlyn felt ashamed and angry and confused. She liked Amy Matthews; in fact, the young widow had been one of the first people she'd met when she arrived in Tillyhenge. They had hit it off from the start and although they hadn't seen much of each other recently, especially with Amy spending so much time at the Manor, Caitlyn had been looking forward to renewing their friendship. Now she felt abashed at her feelings of resentment towards the other girl. If Amy had captured James's heart, shouldn't she have been happy for them?

The tumult of emotions left her feeling raw and uncomfortable, and she took solace in Antoine de Villiers's steady stream of compliments and flirting. Besides, he really was very charming company, even if his flattery was a bit overdone sometimes.

Every so often, she caught Pomona frowning at her but she shrugged it off. It wasn't her fault that she had been forced to change places.

As dessert was being served, there was a lull in the conversation and Pomona said loudly, "James—Caitlyn said she found a weird structure in the grounds today: a sort of tower with a door and nothing inside except a spiral staircase going to the top."

"Oh, that's the Folly," said James with a smile.

"What's it for?"

James chuckled. "Absolutely nothing. They're a classic English eccentricity. As Antoine will probably tell you, the word comes from the French *'folie'*, which means 'madness'—and that is pretty much what people thought of those who built them. A lot of follies were built in the eighteenth century, usually by the wealthy landowners of the time."

"But why build them?" asked Pomona. "I mean, you gotta have a *reason* to build something."

"No, that was the whole point—there was no reason," said James. "In fact, you could say that it was a way to show the power and wealth of a person: that he could spend all this money and labour building something that had absolutely no purpose. And they were usually very whimsical or extravagant in their design too—for instance, built to look like a crumbling castle or a Greek temple... There's even a folly in Dunmore Park in Scotland that's in the shape of a giant pineapple."

"No way!" said Pomona.

James laughed. "Yes. I'll show you a picture of it sometime, if you like. Most of them are a variation of a tower though, like the one here on the estate."

"There's a folly tower in Yorkshire called the Forgotten Folly," one of the guests spoke up. "It was built by an eccentric Yorkshireman so that his servants could look out from the top of the tower and see their master approaching, then run down to ensure that 'dinner was served' as soon as he walked through the door." She giggled. "Personally, I think it's quite nice having such things in our history. It's one of the quirks that makes England so unique and interesting."

"*Mais non*, there are such follies in other countries too," Antoine said. "Several in France and Germany... and even the United States: Belvedere Castle in Central Park, in New York—that is a folly."

"Really?" said Pomona with interest. "I'll need to go see it the next time I'm there." She turned back to James. "So the one here on the estate—have you been inside it?"

"Yes, a couple of times."

"What's in the room at the top?" Caitlyn asked. "The door was locked. I couldn't see inside."

"It's not that interesting," said James with a rueful smile. "If you're imagining something like Bluebeard's room, you'll be disappointed. It's actually just an empty space at the top, with a framework of open archways all around."

"You mean, like a room with no walls?" said Pomona. "Is that, like, part of the wacky folly thing too?"

"Actually, I think this was intended to be a belfry."

Antoine raised his eyebrows. "A belfry?"

"Is there a bell in there?" asked another guest.

James shook his head. "I don't know if there ever was one or if the belfry was never completed—but I've never seen a bell and I don't think there's any record of one in the Folly. Actually, there never used to be a door—just an open doorway at the top of the staircase, leading into the belfry chamber—but my mother found out I was playing in the Folly when I was a child and she was afraid I'd fall off the tower, so she insisted that a door be added. Probably just as well," said James with a chuckle. "It's very exposed up there and a long way down."

"This is all fascinating!" said another guest. "I'd love to see this Folly. Can we go and have a look tomorrow?"

"Certainly. In fact, I was planning to suggest a picnic lunch and a walk around the grounds in the afternoon. We could visit the Folly and then stroll down to the lake and do some boating..."

There were enthusiastic responses from around the table.

"That's great," said James, counting the number of heads. "And we're an even number so that'll be easy for the boats—"

"Ah, do not include me, *mon ami*," said Antoine in a regretful tone. "I am afraid I will not be able to join you."

"Ohhh... why not?" asked one of the female guests, fluttering her eyelashes at him. "We'll miss you, Monsieur de Villiers."

He gave her a perfunctory smile. "Please, call me Antoine," he said smoothly. "And I, too, will miss the pleasure of your company. However, I must make a trip north tomorrow."

"Oh? Everything all right, Antoine?" asked James.

His friend held a hand up. "It is a trifling business I must attend to, but it requires a trip to Birmingham. I will leave mid-morning and I do not think I shall be back in time to join the party."

"Oh. Shame. Well, if you do manage to get back early enough, ask one of the staff to direct you down to the lake."

"*Merci.*" The Frenchman inclined his head.

James rose from the table. "Right. Shall we head back to the Drawing Room for tea and coffee? And chocolates provided by *Bewitched by Chocolate*, of course," he said with a smile.

They drifted back to the luxurious Drawing Room and settled on the beautiful sofa suites and plush armchairs. Caitlyn found a seat at the back of the room and watched in silent enjoyment as a box of chocolate truffles was passed around. She always loved seeing people's faces when they tasted the

Widow Mags's chocolates for the first time.

"Ohhh... this is absolutely delicious!"

"Have you tasted the espresso cup with mocha ganache and dark chocolate shavings? The flavours are incredible."

"No, but the milk chocolate truffle with crunchy English toffee is heavenly—you've got to have one."

"Oh my God, where did you get these chocolates, James? They are divine!"

Amy came and sat down next to Caitlyn. "It's nice seeing people enjoy the chocolates," she said, her eyes twinkling.

"Yes," Caitlyn agreed. Then, feeling guilty for her jealous thoughts earlier, she gave the other woman a big smile and said, "How have you been? I haven't seen you around the village—you must be busy up here at the Manor."

"Yes, although I've also been away a few times," said Amy. "I went to visit my sister in Bath the day before yesterday—the day of the murder, actually. I only got back to Tillyhenge this morning and it was quite a shock hearing the news."

"Oh? So you weren't at the Open-Air Cinema at all?"

"I popped into the Manor late afternoon, just before I left, to check the mail, but I only stayed for half an hour. I could see them setting up on the lawn as I was leaving..." She glanced at Caitlyn curiously. "Do the police have any suspects?"

"They think it's someone who was a recent

arrival to the village—like that new tenant, Lionel Spelling."

"Really? Funny, I actually saw him that afternoon."

Caitlyn sat up straighter. "Where?"

"As I was driving out of the parklands—he was walking along the edge of the driveway, you know, just by the turn-off that leads to the old farmyard and the workers' cottages around the back of the Manor. I suppose he must have been returning home."

"Was he alone?"

"Hmm... actually, there was someone walking a few yards behind him. I'm not sure if they were together."

"Was it a man or a woman? Did you recognise them?"

Amy frowned. "It wasn't anyone I knew. An older man. Very dapper, in a tweed jacket with a red kerchief in the pocket—"

"That sounds like Pierre Rochat!"

Amy looked stunned. "The man who was murdered?"

"Have you told the police about this yet?" Caitlyn asked urgently.

Amy shook her head. "They didn't ask to question me. I suppose because I'd left Tillyhenge before the murder happened and—"

"You must speak to Inspector Walsh tomorrow and tell him what you saw."

Before Amy could reply, James called out from the other side of the room. He was crouched next to a large antique bureau, rummaging in the bottom compartment.

"Amy—do you know where the board games are? They don't seem to be where they're normally stashed. The chaps are asking for a game of Charades."

Several of James's friend gave a cheer. "Hurrah! Charades!"

"Oh, I think they were moved to that cupboard..." said Amy, rising and excusing herself to Caitlyn.

She crossed to the other side of the room and produced the board game, which the rest of the group fell on with another cheer. When she tried to return to Caitlyn's side, however, one of James's male friends grabbed her arm and pulled her down next to him. Soon they were boisterously acting out the first card whilst the others shouted guesses.

Caitlyn watched them contentedly from her quiet corner. A bottle of port had been passed around and she had accepted a generous glass. Now she leaned back against the cushions and sipped the sweet dessert wine. Soon, she felt hot and flushed—what with the champagne before dinner, the wine during dinner, and now the port, she had consumed far more alcohol than she was used to and felt her head swimming slightly. Getting up quietly, she walked to the back of the room, where French doors led out onto the terrace, and wondered if she should open one to let in a bit of fresh air.

"It is very warm, *mademoiselle*, is it not?" said a silky voice beside her.

She turned to see Antoine de Villiers smiling at her. He gestured towards the terrace outside. "I was thinking of taking a stroll—perhaps you'd like to join me?"

Caitlyn hesitated, glancing back into the room. The group was getting quite rowdy. She saw Amy clutching James's arm and laughing as they performed some challenge together.

She turned back to the handsome Frenchman and gave him a bright smile. "Yes, thanks—a walk sounds lovely."

He turned the handle and opened the door, sweeping a hand in front of her. "After you, *mademoiselle*."

Caitlyn threw a last look over her shoulder, then turned and stepped out into the darkness.

CHAPTER EIGHTEEN

Light shone out of the French windows, casting squares of gold along the flagstones. Beyond the terrace, a full moon glowed softly, painting everything in shades of grey and indigo. Caitlyn breathed deeply, enjoying the scent of honeysuckle in the balmy night air as they walked down the terrace and around the Manor. The sounds of talking and laughter became fainter and fainter as they walked farther away, and soon they were deep in the shadows on one side of the house. Here, the temperature was much cooler and Caitlyn shivered as goosebumps rose on her skin.

"You are cold, *cherie*," said Antoine, sliding an arm around her shoulders. The weight of his hand made Caitlyn uncomfortable and she wriggled quickly away.

"I'm all right. Maybe we should go back," she said, turning around.

"*Un moment, mademoiselle*," murmured the Frenchman, walking farther on and looking up at the building next to them. "I have not been to this side of the Manor…"

Caitlyn followed his gaze and recognised the familiar façade. She had been here recently, rescuing a naughty black kitten from a tree.

"This is the back wing of the Manor," she told him. "It's not really used and the Portrait Gallery isn't open to the public."

"Ah… yes, I remember James speaking of the gallery when we were at Oxford… But why is it not part of the tour? I would have thought that it would be of great interest to visitors."

"James didn't seem to think so. He said none of the paintings were by Old Masters or particularly valuable. And besides, I think he wasn't keen for the public to see his father's collection."

"But why? What is in this collection?"

"I don't know… I think the old Lord Fitzroy had a strong interest in magic and witchcraft, but I didn't really see anything when I was in the room. Most of the display cases were covered with white sheets."

"Are you not curious, *mademoiselle*?" asked Antoine with a playful gleam in his eyes.

"Well, yes, but—"

"Is there a way into the Manor from this side?"

"Yes, there's a door behind that bush, there…"

She pointed.

Antoine walked over and Caitlyn followed reluctantly. She was sure the door would be locked but, to her surprise, the handle turned easily under the Frenchman's hand. The door opened, showing a darkened passageway beyond. He gave her a mocking bow and swept a hand in front of her.

"Ladies first."

Caitlyn held back. "I don't think this is a good idea—"

"Come, come, *mademoiselle*—where is your sense of adventure? Or are you afraid of coming into the dark with me?" Antoine raised a teasing eyebrow.

Caitlyn lifted her chin. "Of course I'm not afraid of you."

She hesitated, then stepped through the doorway. She found herself in a familiar stairwell, with a flight of stairs zigzagging upwards. Antoine swept his hand mockingly in front of her again and she led the way up the stairs, stopping at last in front of a thick wooden door decorated with ornate ironwork. The last time she had faced this door, it had been locked and she'd had to use a spell to open it, but she was certainly not going to do that in front of Antoine de Villiers.

But again, to her surprise, the door opened smoothly under his touch; a moment later, they were standing inside, surveying the dusty room. It looked just as she remembered, with a row of oil paintings along one long wall, facing the windows, and various items of furniture scattered around the edges, mostly covered in white sheets.

Antoine walked slowly down the length of the room, looking up at each portrait. "*Alors,* James is not here?"

Caitlyn followed behind him. "No... he said his father wanted him to get a portrait done but he wasn't keen."

Antoine chuckled. "Yes, my friend is very different from his father, *n'est-ce pas?* The old Lord Fitzroy was a slave to tradition whereas James... he favours the modern thinking... and I am in much agreement with him. One can cling to the old ways for too long. Sometimes, one must embrace new methods, new solutions to a problem..."

He was walking slowly as he talked, lifting a sheet every so often to peer beneath, and Caitlyn watched uneasily.

"Maybe we should go," she said. "James and the others must be missing us and—" She broke off as she saw him approach a small painting hanging on a wall at the back of the room. Almost against her will, she went over to join him and looked up at the picture in the antique gilt frame. It depicted four men riding on horses in a bleak landscape. Each horse was a different colour: black, red, white, and pale green, and the men had cruel, stern expressions—all except the last, whose face was hidden by a hood.

"It is an interesting painting, this," Antoine commented. "Do you know who they are?"

"Yes, James told me. They are the Four Horsemen of the Apocalypse. The red one is War, the white one is Plague, the black one is Famine, and that pale green one is Death."

"*Très bien!* Yes, they are the harbingers of the Apocalypse—the end of all time."

"But that's just a legend, isn't it?" said Caitlyn, attempting a light laugh. "They're not real."

"The same way that witches and vampires are not real?"

Caitlyn stared at him.

Antoine turned back to the painting. "It is a curious thing—the legend of the Four Horsemen is familiar around the world, and yet so few details are known. Their names, for instance—nothing is known about the riders' real names... except for the last one." He nodded at the figure with the hood. "The rider of the Pale Horse. His name is known as 'Thanatos'—the Ancient Greek word for 'Death'."

Caitlyn shivered. "You seem to know a lot about them."

Antoine shrugged. "It is only what I read, like everyone else... There is not much information to be found about the Four Horsemen and many have made up their own versions of the truth. This painting is very old... and with such a unique subject matter... I would assume that it is very valuable..." His eyes sharpened and he leaned closer to the painting—so close that his nose was almost touching the oiled surface. "*Diable!*" he murmured. "Can it be...?"

A sound behind them made Caitlyn whirl around. She saw James Fitzroy standing in the doorway of the Portrait Gallery. His grey eyes held an expression of mingled surprise and annoyance, although his tone was carefully neutral as he came in and said:

"Ah... there you are. We were wondering where you had disappeared to."

"We came out for a stroll and I persuaded the lovely Miss Le Fey to give me a private tour of this wing of the Manor," said Antoine, smiling at Caitlyn.

"I'm sorry," said Caitlyn. "I hope we're not trespassing or something. We should really have asked you first—"

"No, no, it's fine," said James shortly. "You know you're welcome to explore anywhere you like in the Manor. It was just that you were gone so long and you hadn't told anyone..."

Antoine made a remorseful face. "It is my fault. I had not intended for us to stay away, but when one is with company such as Miss Le Fey, it is easy to forget the time," he said, placing a possessive hand against the small of her back.

Caitlyn stiffened and she saw James's mouth tighten.

"Yes, well, perhaps we'd better join the others now," he said curtly.

Antoine gave Caitlyn a teasing grin. "Ah, I think perhaps Lord Fitzroy is jealous of me commanding your attention." He laughed and sauntered over to James. "Do not fret, *mon ami*. I return her to you now."

James's cheeks reddened slightly. "That's not what I meant. Caitlyn is her own woman. If she wishes to come out for a stroll with you—" He broke off and cleared his throat. "Anyway, how did you get into this room? The door is normally locked."

"Perhaps one of the staff forgot to lock it?" said Antoine carelessly as he walked through the door.

James frowned and turned to follow him. "That's unlikely. This side of the Manor is rarely used and the staff have very little reason to come here on a daily..."

Their voices faded as they stepped out into the hallway. Caitlyn started to follow, then something made her pause and look back at the painting. Just like the last time she saw it, she was riveted by the way the colours seemed to glow on the canvas— almost as if they were freshly applied. She narrowed her eyes, taking in details she hadn't noticed the first time. The landscape behind the riders wasn't as barren as she had first thought: in the distance, a thick forest spread out like a dark green blanket, covering the land... and there, in the corner of the canvas behind the Pale Horse... something peeked out amongst the trees...

Caitlyn moved closer and squinted... it was hard

to make out the details but it looked like a tower, with a flock of something dark encircling it... birds?

Bats, Caitlyn realised. And at the same time, she realised something else. The tower looked familiar. In fact, she had seen one exactly like it that morning: the Folly of Huntingdon Manor.

CHAPTER NINETEEN

Caitlyn's first thought when she woke up the next morning was of Viktor. Despite Bertha's and the Widow Mags's assurances, she was worried about the old vampire. She decided to head over to *Bewitched by Chocolate* as soon as breakfast was over and see if he had turned up—if not, she was going to insist on a search party to comb the woods around Gertrude Smith's cottage.

But when she and Pomona arrived at the chocolate shop an hour later, Caitlyn was delighted to find Viktor seated at the wooden table in the kitchen with her aunt and her grandmother.

"Viktor! You're all right!" she cried, running up to him. She looked with concern at his arm, which was bandaged and in a sling. "Are you badly hurt? Did that terrier bite through your wing?"

"I'm fine, I'm fine," Viktor blustered, waving her

off.

"He did have quite a bad tear in the wing membrane," Bertha said. "But don't worry—I've applied a herbal compress and it will heal quickly."

"But dog bites can turn really nasty," said Caitlyn. "It's all the bacteria in their mouths. You can get blood poisoning or some other horrible infection. I think you should go to hospital and get a shot of antibiotics—"

"I am not going to hospital for something as trivial as a dog bite!" cried Viktor. "Young lady, I'll have you know, as an Ancient Guardian Protector, I am well seasoned in battle and used to dealing with wounds of far more serious nature! Why, when I was a young vampire, I once fought a werewolf single-handed—"

"Yes, but this is different!" said Caitlyn. "You can't expect to just rebound like you did then."

"And why not?"

"Well, because you're—" Caitlyn broke off, not wanting to say: "Because you're *old* now."

Bertha said gently, "The herbal compress contains strong anti-bacterial compounds, which should stop any infection. In any case, Viktor's vampire regenerative abilities mean that the wound will heal before infection has time to take hold." She reached over and carefully unwound a section of bandage. "There, see? It's already healing over."

Caitlyn leaned over to look and was impressed. The deep gash had sealed and the skin already looked pink and healthy. "Wow... what's in the compress?"

"Oh, a few special herbs, mixed to a specific recipe... and a little bit of magic to bind it all together," said Bertha with a smile.

The Widow Mags gave Viktor a severe look. "If you hadn't been so greedy, you wouldn't be in this position in the first place. Always thinking about your stomach... Stealing from a fruit bowl—*really*, Viktor!"

The old vampire looked sulky. "I only wanted to inspect the interior of the cottage—Caitlyn wouldn't let me go in with her, so I had to creep in the back myself. Then I saw the bananas and they smelled so delicious..." He flexed his arm. "Anyway, I shall be back in the air in no time."

"Can you really change into a bat?" Pomona spoke up for the first time.

The old vampire looked at her in surprise. "But of course. I can shift into other creatures too, but a bat is my preferred form. A fruit bat, to be precise."

"But... you don't *look* like a shape-shifter," said Pomona, eyeing him suspiciously. "Or even a vampire, actually."

"And how am I supposed to look?"

"Well... like... handsome and *hot*..." Pomona muttered. Then she brightened. "Oh, you must have been old already when you were turned."

"Turned?" Viktor looked at her in puzzlement. "Turned where?"

"Turned into a vampire," explained Pomona.

"I wasn't turned into a vampire!" cried Viktor, scandalised. "I was born one."

"Born? You can be born a vampire?"

"Of course. It is something that runs in certain families."

Pomona furrowed her brow. "You mean, like a genetic mutation?"

"I am not a mutation! Vampirism is... a rare 'gift' or a talent, that appears in some babies born within certain families. Like red hair," he said, glancing at Caitlyn's head. "Or the ability to have perfect pitch or to draw beautifully—"

Pomona frowned. "So you were born with fangs?"

"No, the vampiric trait is not immediately apparent—it develops as we grow older and enter puberty. But even before then, those of us who are vampires know instinctively that we are different from others. The trait is also inconsistent—like red hair." He glanced at Caitlyn's head again. "It can sometimes skip several generations and there is no predicting when it will appear again, if at all. In fact, in recent centuries, there have been fewer and fewer vampires born. In centuries past, vampires were numerous and powerful, but our numbers have been dwindling. We are a dying race." Viktor sighed heavily, suddenly looking his six hundred and thirty-four years.

"You mean, vampires are going extinct?" asked Caitlyn in dismay.

"Yes," Bertha answered. "If nothing is done and the rates of vampire births continue to decline, soon there may not be any vampires at all."

"But I don't get it—instead of just waiting for it to randomly pop up in a family somewhere, why can't you just, like, marry each other and make vampire babies?" asked Pomona.

Viktor drew back in horror. "Vampires do not marry! For those of us who have been blessed with this gift, we honour it by taking a life of celibacy. Vampires were once the Ancient Guardians of the Underworld, tasked with protecting the vulnerable and keeping order in the magical realms. We devote our lives to that duty," he said proudly. "In any case, vampires are always males—the trait is passed down through the male line. So there would be no female vampires to marry, even had we wanted to."

"So there's really no other way to become a vampire?" asked Pomona disbelievingly. "All that stuff in the movies and books about being turned into a vampire after being bitten isn't true?"

Viktor hesitated. "There *is* some truth in that," he said at last. "Yes, there is a second way that vampires can be created but it is a cruel, despicable act, forced upon the innocent without their consent." He scowled. "I have seen it happen in my time, when an immoral vampire preys on young boys. They are bitten and infected with an unnatural thirst for blood. In this way, they become 'vampires' but they are nothing like real vampires. They are tortured monsters, condemned to a life of savagery as they hunt for their next victim. They are the ones who have inspired the stories of horror and fear in human history, and those books and movies you speak of. True vampires—those who came to it by birthright and who respect the ancient order— follow a strict code of honour. We would never hurt another human being. We are protectors, not killers."

"But... what about when you feed?" asked Pomona. "Don't you have to hurt humans when you suck their blood?"

"Vampires do not feed on blood! That is yet another myth perpetrated by those ridiculous books and films. We follow a diet determined by our bat form, and that is determined in turn by the families we are descended from. My family, for instance, came from the Order Megachiroptera: vampires born in my family shift into fruit bats, and therefore I am a fruitarian."

"But I heard that most bats eat insects," said Pomona, making a face. "Does that mean that most vampires munch on bugs?"

"There is nothing wrong with an insectivorous diet," said Viktor huffily. "Insects are full of protein. It is very good for you. There are also those belonging to Orders which consume small mammals, birds, lizards, and frogs."

"Lizards?" said Pomona. "Eeeuuggghh!"

"But you told me there *are* some vampires who feed on blood," Caitlyn said.

"Yes, that is right," Viktor conceded. "A small number of families belong to the Order Vampyrus—their members shift into vampire bats and enjoy the taste of blood. But not necessarily human blood," he added sternly. "You can feed on blood and never choose a human as a victim."

"But you could get some evil vampire dude who doesn't wanna follow the old code of honour," said Pomona. "And maybe that's who killed Pierre Rochat! That would explain the puncture wounds in his neck and how his body was drained of blood—"

"I still think Inspector Walsh is right and Rochat was murdered because of his criminal connections," interrupted Caitlyn.

"Maybe the two things aren't separate," said Pomona.

"What do you mean?"

"Well, maybe the criminal guy—the ringleader—is a vampire as well!"

Caitlyn rolled her eyes. "First you thought he was a butler and a criminal... now you think he could be a butler and a criminal *and* a vampire?"

"Why not?" said Pomona. "It's, like, you're a bookworm and a witch and a redhead. You can be multiple things at the same time."

"I suppose... It just seems like too much of a coincidence," said Caitlyn. "And anyway, it doesn't make sense. Supposing the murderer *was* the ringleader—and happened to be a vampire—why would he murder Pierre Rochat? Rochat was his partner in crime, who was going to help him get rid of the stolen jewellery. There's no reason to kill him."

"Maybe he got hungry when they were exchanging the jewels and decided to chomp on Rochat instead."

"That's the dumbest idea I've ever heard!" said Caitlyn, exasperated.

"Oh yeah? You got a better one?" Pomona shot back.

The Widow Mags had been silently watching the girls argue back and forth, but now the old witch spoke up:

"I agree with Caitlyn. The answer lies in the reason Pierre Rochat came to Tillyhenge."

"To meet the ringleader of the jewellery thieves—I'm sure of that," Caitlyn said. "It's just too much of a coincidence otherwise, for a robbery to have occurred in London recently, for the ringleader to be hiding in this area of the Cotswolds and for Rochat—a fence who disposes of stolen jewels—to come to this tiny village."

"What was stolen in the robbery?" asked Bertha. "Perhaps that can give us a clue."

Caitlyn frowned thoughtfully. "Well, the biggest thing was a pink diamond. It's worth hundreds of thousands of pounds... Oh! And I just remembered. There was something else: Inspector Walsh mentioned an antique silver bloodstone brooch."

"A bloodstone brooch?" The Widow Mags looked up.

Caitlyn nodded. "It caught my attention because of the Fitzroys' bloodstone ring that was stolen recently. Although Inspector Walsh insists that they're not related. This one is just a plain bloodstone—there is no engraving on it—and it's set in a brooch in the shape of a key."

"A key? Oh my Goddess, maybe it's *the* key!" said Bertha. "The key for the belfry!"

Viktor snorted. "That is a bedtime story told to vampire children!"

"It may not be just a bedtime story," said the Widow Mags quietly.

Caitlyn looked from one to the other in confusion.

"What belfry?" asked Pomona. "What are you guys talking about?"

Bertha turned to her. "Have you heard the expression 'bats in the belfry'?"

"Yeah, it means someone is crazy or nuts."

"That's not actually its original meaning. It's been corrupted through use in human societies, who have no real understanding of its origin. The phrase comes from an ancient legend passed down in vampire lore and often told in vampire families. A bit like your stories of 'Cinderella' or 'Little Red Riding Hood'," said Bertha with a smile. "It's said that there is an enchanted key which, when used to unlock a certain belfry tower, can transform it into a magical structure, one that's linked to the Other Realms. Then, when you go inside the belfry, you'll find a magical bell. If this is rung, it has the power to summon a swarm of bats to the belfry—the basis of a great army... a vampire army."

"Bah! What load of garlic!" cried Viktor. "It is just like the silly legend about the pot of gold at the end of the rainbow. I know a poor leprechaun who has spent his life searching for that gold—but has anyone ever seen it? It is a myth—just like the bats in the belfry!"

"There may be more truth to the legend than you think," said the Widow Mags grimly. "And in any case, the lure of such a prize may be enough to be dangerous. There are many vampires worried about the vampire race dying out, who are frustrated by the 'old ways'. They are not willing to wait for the Fates to decide when the next vampire is to be born—they want to take matters into their own hands—and the legend of the 'bats in the belfry' is a very seductive one. It suggests a way for the vampire race to regain its strength and to dominate the world once more."

"But such an army... they would not be true vampires," said Viktor, aghast. "They would be an army of the undead, such as I described earlier: savage and monstrous, with no compassion or decency. Surely no vampire would dream of unleashing such a plague on humanity!"

"You may cling to the old ways, Viktor, and be bound by a code of honour, but not all vampires are like you. Especially the younger ones, who have been born in the modern age... they care little for the old standards of nobility and decency. For them, the end is worth any cost. They would rather have bloodthirsty monster vampires than no vampires at all. And with such an army, vampires could dominate the world once more."

There was a long silence as everyone pondered the Widow Mags's grim words.

"But that hasn't happened yet, right?" asked Pomona. "Which means the key is still safe. As long as no one finds this antique brooch with the key, they can't call up some creepy vampire army."

"You're assuming this key is real!" said Caitlyn. "It might all be just a story. And even if it isn't, that doesn't mean that *this* antique brooch that was stolen *is* the magical key. I think you're assuming way too much."

"Okay, but I still think the murderer is a vampire," said Pomona, shooting Caitlyn a defiant look. "Whatever Inspector Walsh says. There's just, like, too many clues pointing in that direction, too many coincidences. I mean, we've got this vampire legend... we've got an antique brooch in the shape of a key... we've got a dead guy with fang marks in his neck... *C'mon!* There's gotta be a vampire involved!"

"I think Pomona is right," said Bertha. "I think

there are too many coincidences to ignore."

Caitlyn looked at the Widow Mags for support, but the old witch said nothing. She turned back to Pomona.

"Okay… assuming you're right and the murderer is a vampire—how does that help us find out who it is?"

"Well, that's easy!" Pomona exclaimed. "If the murderer is a vampire, then we just need to figure out who could be a vampire and that would give us a shortlist, right? I know!" She turned to Viktor excitedly. "Can't you go around and look at people in the village and tell?"

"Tell what, young lady?" asked Viktor.

"Tell if they're a vampire!"

"It is not always obvious."

"Why not? I mean, shouldn't vampires know each other?"

Viktor gave her an irate look. "Young lady, when you walk into a room and look at a group of people, can you tell everyone who is American?"

"I…" Pomona faltered. "Well, if they dress a certain way or speak with a loud American accent… Yeah, okay, I see what you mean. I wouldn't be able to tell if they're, like, really trying to hide it."

"It is the same for vampires. Yes, I can recognise those of my kind—but not if they make an effort to disguise it." Viktor sighed. "And this murderer is clever; he will be making every effort to conceal who he really is."

CHAPTER TWENTY

Caitlyn was still mulling over everything that Viktor, Bertha, and the Widow Mags had told her, as she and Pomona drove back to the Manor later that morning. She wondered if she could ask James to unlock the door at the top of the Folly and have a look in the belfry chamber when they visited it later.

"Maybe we can ask James to look in the Folly this afternoon," said Pomona, obviously sharing her thoughts. "I mean, if we're talking about coincidences, it's a pretty big fat coincidence that there's a tower with a belfry right here in the same village that Pierre Rochat was murdered. It's gotta be connected!"

"Pomie, I just thought of something," said Caitlyn. "When I was with Antoine in the Portrait Gallery last night, I had a look at that painting again—you know, the one I told you about, with the Four Horsemen... and I noticed something in the background: a tower in the middle of a forest, with a swarm of bats flying around it."

"Holy guacamole!" said Pomona. "That's, like, proof! Why didn't you say something earlier?"

"I didn't think of it. But it's not really proof of anything—I mean, the person who painted that picture might have heard of the vampire legend and just put it in there for fun. Still... the tower in the painting does look exactly like the one on the Fitzroy estate."

"You see?" said Pomona, getting so excited that the car swerved slightly. "That *is* proof, Caitlyn! Or at least it's a clue—it means that the Fitzroy Folly could be the tower in the legend. And I'll bet you anything that the stolen antique brooch *is* the enchanted key that unlocks the magical belfry. We need to tell James and—oh crap!" She made a sound of annoyance. "I took a wrong turn. We're on that big road heading south, instead of the side one that goes to Huntingdon Manor."

Caitlyn saw a road sign whizz past and realised that Pomona was right. They had ended up on the A429, otherwise known as the Fosse Way—an ancient Roman road built during the Iron Age—which was one of the main roads cutting north-south through the Cotswolds. It eventually merged with the bigger motorway that led all the way to London. Thankfully, it wasn't one of the dual carriageway roads with a central barrier that prevented easy turning.

"It's okay—you just need to find a turning lane and a side road, and you can head back the way we came," said Caitlyn.

Pomona adjusted her speed to match the other cars and cruised along, looking for a turning lane.

"You know, I think I'm getting the hang of driving on the left side of the road. It's just—" She broke off suddenly and stared through the windscreen. "Hey! Isn't that Antoine de Villiers?"

Caitlyn looked around. "Where?"

"There! In that green convertible up ahead."

Caitlyn caught a glimpse of the handsome Frenchman. "Oh... you're right, that *is* him... He said he was going somewhere for business today, didn't he?"

"Yeah, but look at the direction he's travelling in."

"What do you mean?"

"Well, we're heading south."

"So?"

"So yesterday at dinner, he said he was going to Birmingham. That's north, right?"

"Maybe he changed his plans."

Pomona said nothing. A minute later, a turning lane appeared on their right but she didn't slow down.

"Hey—you're going to miss the turn off..." said Caitlyn.

Pomona kept her foot on the accelerator. "I'm gonna follow Antoine."

"You're going to what?"

"I wanna see where he's going."

Caitlyn exhaled in exasperation. "What does it matter where he's going?"

"He lied yesterday. I wanna know why."

"Pomie, this is ridiculous!"

But Pomona ignored her and kept her foot steadily on the gas, keeping Antoine's car in sight but making sure that she wasn't too close. Soon they were on the A40, passing through the ring road around Oxford and then joining the M40—the main motorway down to London.

"You're not going to just keep following him, are you?" asked Caitlyn incredulously.

"Why not? England is pretty small—I could drive from here down to Brighton on the south coast in, like, two hours. Anyway, I bet he's going to London."

Pomona turned out to be right. An hour later, they were on the outskirts of London, navigating the busier roads leading into the capital city. It was harder now to keep a safe distance behind Antoine de Villiers without losing him, and they almost did at one set of traffic lights, which turned red just as he crossed over.

"You just drove through a red light!" gasped Caitlyn as her cousin floored the accelerator and horns sounded angrily around them.

Pomona shrugged, her face a picture of concentration. It had become a game for her, following Antoine to his destination—a game she was determined not to lose. Caitlyn was relieved when the green sportscar finally slowed down, looking for a place to park. If they had followed Antoine any longer, she shuddered to think how many traffic infringements Pomona might've racked up!

Farther up the street, Caitlyn recognised the majestic façade of Harrods, one of the world's largest and most famous department stores. They were in the elite London neighbourhood of Knightsbridge. Antoine de Villiers turned into a side road and Pomona carefully followed, driving casually past him as he pulled into a free parking spot.

"Jeez—how did he find a spot so easily?" she muttered.

Thankfully, luck was on their side too, and they found a free space a moment later. Pomona slid the car haphazardly into the spot, then sprang out of the car.

"Come on!" she urged Caitlyn. "We've got to see where he's going!"

They jogged to where the Frenchman had parked his car and were just in time to see him in the distance, walking rapidly. They followed and soon came back out onto the larger street where Harrods was situated. In fact, Antoine de Villiers seemed to be heading straight for the luxury department store. He paused outside the grand main entrance and exchanged a word with one of the famous Harrods doormen, dressed in the iconic forest-green-and-gold livery, before disappearing into the store.

"C'mon!" said Pomona, putting on a burst of speed.

They hurried through the double doors and joined the crowds milling in the maze of sprawling shopping halls. Both girls strained to keep Antoine in view. Inside the vast store, with over three hundred departments across a million square feet, they would probably never find the Frenchman again if they lost sight of him.

Antoine was obviously familiar with Harrods, moving swiftly past the luxury accessories and perfumes, through the famous Egyptian room, decorated in gold fixtures and pillars carved with hieroglyphics, and on to the legendary Food Hall. The girls followed, darting between the aisles as they tried to stay close but unseen. It was hard walking past the incredible displays of gourmet food without being tempted—especially as it was now lunchtime and both girls' stomachs were rumbling. Even Pomona became distracted from her mission as she slowed and hovered next to the display cases.

"Omigod, check out those chocolate cakes... and those pink ones shaped like little rosebuds... and the macaroons! And did you see those gorgeous tiny cupcakes? Oh, wait, the English call them fairy cakes... I wish we could stop and taste some! Omigod, look... there's like a million different sausages here... champagne ham... wow, so many pies—I've never heard of these flavours: 'Royal Game with Blackcurrants'... 'Hazelnut and Truffle Oil'... Man, I'm starving now! Wow, they've even got foreign stuff too... 'A Taste of India'... sushi and noodles... Mmm... French pastries and baguettes... *'Amaretti'*—Italian almond cookies... ooh, and *speculaas*! I had some the night of the Open-Air Cinema—they're delicious... Hah—they've got a Krispy Kreme Doughnuts stand—can you believe it?"

Caitlyn glanced anxiously ahead. "We're going to lose Antoine if we don't keep moving."

Pomona sighed and gave a last lingering look at the shelves, then turned and hurried on. As they rounded a corner, however, they nearly collided with the man himself. He was standing next to the Caviar House & Oyster Bar, looking down at his phone.

"Do you think he just came in here to grab a bite to eat?" Pomona asked in disappointment.

The Frenchman looked up and the girls jerked out of sight.

"Did he see us?" hissed Pomona.

"No, I don't think so," whispered Caitlyn.

Cautiously, they peeked around the corner of the aisle, then relaxed slightly. Antoine de Villiers had walked on again, past the seafood bar and through an adjoining archway to the hall beyond. The girls followed. They found themselves stepping into a spacious hallway in which a large group of people were gathered. Unlike the crowds milling about in the other halls, this group didn't seem to be browsing but rather waiting for something.

"What's going on?" asked Pomona.

"I don't know… it looks like there's some kind of event…" said Caitlyn, stretching up on tiptoe to peer over the heads of those around them.

She could see some members of the press hovering around, brandishing cameras with huge flashbulbs, and a few large posters at the sides of the hall. Beckoning Pomona to follow her, she sidled through the crowd until she was standing in front of one of the posters. It depicted a close-up of an exquisitely-cut diamond ring, sparkling against a black velvet background, and some words in elegant calligraphy centred above the image.

"…biennial exhibition in the Harrods Fine Jewellery Room…" Pomona read. She turned to Caitlyn excitedly. "Antoine's come to a jewellery exhibition. This can't be a coincidence!"

CHAPTER TWENTY-ONE

Caitlyn felt a stab of disappointment. She really hadn't wanted to think that Antoine de Villiers could be involved with the murder, but she had to admit that Pomona was right: it did seem like a strange coincidence.

"Where is he?" Pomona asked.

Caitlyn surveyed the area and spotted the Frenchman at the other end of the hallway, next to a set of closed doors which obviously led into the exhibition. He was standing in an area roped off from the rest of the crowd, and from the look of the well-dressed men and women around him, they were obviously members of London's wealthy set— probably enjoying special VIP access to the exhibition before the public was let in. They were being served champagne and canapés whilst they waited for the doors to open and Caitlyn saw several ladies surround Antoine, eagerly vying for his attention.

A separate queue was forming next to the VIP section, with a smartly-dressed young man checking people's names against a list before letting them join the line.

"Look..." Caitlyn pointed out the young man to Pomona. "It looks like it's invitation only."

Her cousin didn't seem daunted. She marched up to the young man and gave him a big smile. He blinked, looking slightly dazzled.

"Can I help you?" he asked politely.

"Ohhh... I hope you can..." Pomona purred. "We were just wondering if we could get in to see the exhibition."

He gave her a regretful look. "I'm so sorry—there are only a limited number of tickets and they were sold out months ago."

"Aww... come on... I know you guys always keep a couple of tickets aside ..." She fluttered her eyelashes and gave him another beguiling smile. "Can't you, like, bend the rules a bit?"

"Well, we do have a few spare tickets, just in case of a celebrity visit or something... but I don't hold them. You'll have to speak to Miss Fothergill. She's the organising secretary for the exhibition and she controls everything." He nodded to a woman standing a few yards away.

Caitlyn glanced over and saw an older woman in

a turtleneck sweater and grey pencil skirt, with a pair of horn-rimmed glasses dangling from a chain around her neck. Her mouth was pursed primly and she stood very erect as she made notes in a leather organiser. Caitlyn didn't think she had ever seen anyone less likely to "bend the rules a bit".

Once again, however, Pomona seemed undaunted. She strolled over to the woman and, leaning close, said warmly, "I had to come and tell you... I just love that top you're wearing!"

"Why, thank you," said Miss Fothergill in surprise, her cheeks flushing with pleasure.

"Is it cashmere? You just can't beat cashmere, can you? But I think you wear it *so* well—I mean, I've seen people do cashmere turtlenecks and they just look kinda 'dated', you know? It totally turned me off—but now that I've seen the way you wear it, it's totally changed my view about turtlenecks!"

Caitlyn didn't know whether to roll her eyes or applaud. Her cousin was outrageous—and yet somehow people seemed to respond to her. Maybe it was Pomona's warm, bubbly manner—or maybe it was because she said everything with such conviction. Confidence was infectious and people often followed exactly where you led them.

"You're from the States, aren't you?" Miss Fothergill asked with a smile.

"California girl, born and bred," said Pomona, tossing her blonde hair over her shoulder.

"Oh, how lovely. I hear the weather there is

wonderful."

"Well, I gotta say, your weather's pretty awesome too. Man, everyone told me it rains all the time in England, but so far it's been fantastic."

"Oh, yes, English summers can be quite nice," said the woman with typical British understatement. "Have you been seeing the sights?"

"Yeah, we've been to some of the big stuff—like the Tower Bridge and the London Dungeons... We haven't had a proper cup of tea yet though."

"You haven't?" The woman looked horrified. "You can't come to England and not experience the full English Afternoon Tea!"

"Oh... is there anywhere you recommend? I know I can trust your taste."

Miss Fothergill's chest puffed up with pride. "Well, there are so many places really—there's the Tea Room here at Harrods, on the fourth floor... that's quite nice... and there's Fortnum & Mason, of course, the famous food emporium in Picadilly— their High Tea is renowned... and if you're going to the Cotswolds, you could have some wonderful afternoon tea in many of the little tearooms in the villages dotted around."

"That sounds awesome," said Pomona. Then she glanced across at the queue and said casually, "By the way, do you know if there are any tickets left for the exhibition? I didn't know it was today and I'm just *dying* to see it!"

"No, I'm afraid all the tickets are sold-out." Miss

Fothergill glanced at her watch and lowered her voice. "But I'll tell you what—we usually keep a few tickets back in case of any last-minute special guests. It's so late now, I don't think anyone else will be coming, so... here you are." She reached into her handbag and withdrew a heavy cream envelope.

Pomona beamed. "Oh, I could kiss you!"

Miss Fothergill looked slightly alarmed. "Er... no, that won't be necessary. But you're welcome." She gave Pomona a prim smile. "It's been lovely chatting to you. I hope you enjoy the rest of your stay in England."

"I don't believe it," said Caitlyn as they hurried to join the queue. "If you ever need a job, Pomie, you'd be great as a door-to-door salesman!"

The VIP crowd had already gone into the exhibition room and the two girls shuffled impatiently at the back of the queue.

"What if Antoine leaves again before we get in?" asked Pomona, craning her neck to look at the open doors ahead.

"Don't worry—he'll probably come out of the same doors so we'll see him. Anyway, the line is starting to move; I think they're letting us in."

Several minutes later, she and Pomona walked into the inner hall and joined the people milling around the displays. Despite the dimmed lights, the whole room seemed to glitter and sparkle as the precious stones within the glass cases caught the spotlights and reflected them back in a shimmer of rainbow colours. Their size and brilliance were breath-taking. For a moment, Caitlyn almost forgot why she was there as she paused beside a glass counter displaying a stunning sapphire-and-diamond necklace on a bed of black velvet.

"He's over there!" Pomona hissed suddenly.

Caitlyn jerked her head up and looked in the direction her cousin was pointing. Antoine de Villiers was standing in the far corner, next to a display case of antique watches. He had his back to them and seemed to be talking to someone.

"Who's he talking to?" asked Pomona, stretching on tiptoe. With the dim ambient lighting, the edges of the room remained in shadow and it was impossible to see.

"Come on!" said Pomona, grabbing Caitlyn's arm and starting to push her way through the crowd.

They jostled and shoved as politely as they could, trying to make their way to the other end of the room as fast as possible. But when they stumbled through the final knot of people and stopped by the antique watch case, they were disappointed to find that Antoine was no longer there. In fact, they could just see his dark head moving slowly away through the crowd.

Pomona made a noise of frustration and was about to plunge after him when the crowd shifted and a tall, dark-haired man walked past them. He was dressed all in black—a perfectly tailored black suit with a black shirt and a black silk tie—and flanked by two hulking bodyguards.

Caitlyn looked up, gasping as she recognised the piercing blue eyes in the thin, cruelly handsome face.

It was Thane Blackmort.

CHAPTER TWENTY-TWO

"Thane!" cried Pomona, her face lighting up. "So good to see you again!" She rushed towards him and stretched up to peck him on the cheek.

So this is the enigmatic Thane Blackmort, Caitlyn thought. Known by the press as 'The Black Tycoon' for his quirky habit of always wearing black, travelling in a black private jet, and only drinking black vodka, Blackmort had risen seemingly out of nowhere to become one of the wealthiest and most powerful men in the world. She had seen brief mentions of him in the press—his bodyguards ensured that the paparazzi never got close enough to get much of a story—but she had heard longer accounts of him from Pomona, who had met him at a London party a few months ago and seemed completely infatuated by his sex appeal.

Looking at the man in the flesh now, Caitlyn had to admit that Pomona's description of him hadn't been wrong—there was something mesmerising about Thane Blackmort. It wasn't just his saturnine good looks or debonair appearance—there was a sense of power, an "aura" to the man that Caitlyn couldn't define.

"Pomona." Blackmort turned his head slightly so that his lips brushed Pomona's cheek, but he never took his eyes off Caitlyn, who shifted uneasily under that piercing blue gaze.

His voice was deep and gravelly, with an accent that Caitlyn couldn't quite place. It wasn't British, it wasn't American, it wasn't European or Australian or Canadian or like any other accent she had ever heard.

"Thane, this is my cousin, Caitlyn Le Fey." Pomona gestured carelessly to Caitlyn. "Omigod, I'm so happy to run into you here! When did you get back to London? Are you staying long?"

"Just for a few days." He paused, then said abruptly, "I am having a private party in my suite. You must come. My limousine is waiting below."

Caitlyn noted the commanding language and tone. This was a man who was used to giving orders and being obeyed. It rankled her slightly and she said, more sharply than she intended:

"I'm afraid we can't. We've already got plans for this afternoon—in fact, we're already missing a lunch date. We should be leaving now to head back." She looked pointedly at Pomona.

Her cousin glanced at Blackmort and bit her lip. "Ohhh..."

"Stay," he said to Pomona, who seemed to melt under that piercing blue gaze.

She turned to Caitlyn and handed her the car keys. "You go," she said.

"What?"

"James won't really mind me not being there," said Pomona. "I can always see the grounds and go boating another time—"

"But Pomie—"

"You should stay too," said Blackmort, turning to her.

Caitlyn looked up into those vivid blue eyes—so blue that they looked almost unreal—and felt the full force of the man's charisma. For a second, she was almost compelled to do as he said, then she frowned, resisting the urge. She saw his eyes flicker and a hint of surprise cross his face.

"No, thank you," she said coolly. "I appreciate the invitation but I need to get back to the Cotswolds."

Blackmort said nothing, although his blue eyes swept over her. Then he inclined his head—a strange, regal gesture—and said softly, "In that case, I hope to have the pleasure of your company some other time... Caitlyn."

The sound of her name on his lips made the hairs stand up on the back of her neck, although she didn't know why. Caitlyn shook off the thought.

I'm imagining it, she told herself. She was being beguiled by the air of mystique surrounding Blackmort—but that was nothing more than a lot of hot air created by the media. He was just a very rich, very good-looking man, who was used to getting his own way—and he had been startled when she had resisted the force of his personality...

Caitlyn glanced at her cousin, annoyed with her—and slightly surprised. Pomona was no pushover. Nor did she normally ditch people at the last minute for a better offer. Although she might have looked like a blonde airhead, Caitlyn knew that her cousin was no shallow social butterfly— Pomona had a strong sense of ethics and integrity. So this kind of behaviour was not like her.

"Pomona..." she started to try again, then sighed and gave up. Her cousin wasn't even looking at her—she had eyes only for Blackmort. "Okay... well, I'm going now... Um... if I take the car, how are you going to get back to Tillyhenge?"

Pomona waved a hand. "Oh, I can get a taxi..."

"From London? It'll cost a fortune!" Caitlyn said. She knew that, like her, Pomona had a large trust fund set up by her celebrity mother and money had never been an issue. Still, her cousin wasn't normally extravagant.

"I guess I'll get the train to Oxford, then, and get a taxi from there."

Caitlyn frowned. "It's not a good idea to travel alone on the trains late at night. How late are you going to be?"

"I don't know." Pomona glanced at Blackmort and giggled. "I guess it depends on how good the party is." She turned back to Caitlyn. "Oh, quit worrying! I'll be fine! If it gets too late, I'll get a room in London. I'm a big girl now and I don't need you to babysit me!"

Caitlyn was left with no choice, and a few minutes later she was retracing their steps, wandering slowly back through the Harrods Food Hall alone. She wondered fleetingly where Antoine de Villiers was—somehow, she had completely forgotten him after meeting Blackmort—but in any case, she was unlikely to catch up with him now. Instead, she stopped at a few of the counters to pick up something to eat on the drive back to Tillyhenge.

As she walked past the aisle where all the cookies were displayed, Caitlyn paused by the packet of traditional Dutch biscuits—*speculaas*—and stared at them thoughtfully. Suddenly, she remembered what Pomona had said earlier: *"...I had some the night of the Open-Air Cinema—they're delicious..."*

How had her cousin managed to get *speculaas* at the Open-Air Cinema? They weren't the type of thing that was sold everywhere and she was surprised that Pomona even knew their name. On an impulse, she pulled out her phone and called her cousin. Pomona was notorious for not hearing her own phone ring because it was always lost at the bottom of her handbag or something similar, but to Caitlyn's relief, this time she answered.

"Pomona?"

"Yeah?" There was giggling in the background, along with several excited voices. It sounded like the party had already started wherever Pomona was.

"Listen, Pomie—you know you were talking about *speculaas* earlier in the Food Hall... How did you know about them?"

"Huh? Whaddya mean?"

"I mean—you said you tasted them on the night of the cinema. Where did you get them from?"

"Uh... oh, that guy, Rochat, gave me some."

Caitlyn jerked upright. "Rochat? Pierre Rochat?"

"Mmm..." Pomona's voice faded and Caitlyn could hear her yelling something to someone in the background, then giggling wildly as music blared from loudspeakers somewhere.

"Pomona!" she said sharply. "This is important!"

Her cousin came back on the line. "Huh? Oh, yeah... sorry. Pierre Rochat had some with him and he offered me a couple. They were really good— freshly baked."

Freshly baked.

Caitlyn's thoughts whirled. Surely it couldn't be...?

"Uh... Caitlyn? I gotta go. They're doing this champagne fountain thing—"

"Okay. Have a good time."

Caitlyn hung up and stared at the phone for a

moment, then she gathered her purchases and made her way out of the department store. Back at the car, she dumped the food on the seat next to her, took a couple of hasty bites of a sandwich, then started the car and began navigating her way out of London. She drove on autopilot, munching and thinking furiously.

Traditional Dutch biscuits weren't common—it was unlikely that Rochat had come to Tillyhenge with some in his pocket. So he must have been given the biscuits *after* arriving in the village... and there was one person she knew who had been making freshly baked *speculaas*.

Gertrude Smith.

CHAPTER TWENTY-THREE

Caitlyn felt her mind whirling. Could they have been looking the wrong way all along? If Rochat got the *speculaas* from Gertrude Smith, did that mean that when Amy Matthews saw him walking in the direction of the workers' cottages, he hadn't been going to Lionel Spelling's place—he had been going next door?

But why? Was Gertrude Smith the person Rochat had been planning to meet in Tillyhenge? Could she have been the ringleader of the jewellery thieves? Caitlyn shook her head in disbelief. That was a crazy idea. She couldn't think of anyone less likely to be a criminal than that stolid, middle-aged Englishwoman with her wellington boots, her yappy terrier, and her gardening obsession.

And yet...

Maybe that was the point. Maybe those elements were all part of the perfect disguise, so that people *wouldn't* suspect her. Caitlyn thought back to the day she had visited Gertrude Smith—something had struck her as slightly odd when she looked at the cottage. At the time, she hadn't been able to put her finger on it, but now as she conjured up the image in her mind's eye—the shiny new gumboots, gleaming spades and trowels, the pretty gloves in a floral fabric—she realised what it was. Everything had been so *clean*, so new, so shiny... If Gertrude really was as keen a gardener as she claimed, surely those spades and trowels, those pretty floral gloves, would have been covered in dirt?

They're props, Caitlyn thought suddenly. She was sure of it. In fact, now she also remembered Old Palmer grumbling about how Gertrude Smith didn't know that azaleas needed acidic soil. Only a true gardener like him would have picked up on details like that—the rest of the world had been easily fooled by her clever disguise.

And then Caitlyn remembered something else. When Rocco the terrier had been turned to chocolate, Gertrude had seemed more selfishly concerned with the fact that she had lost her "brilliant guard dog" than with the dog's well-being. Why would she care so much about having a guard dog—unless there was something valuable she needed to keep guarded?

Such as the stolen jewels.

Yes, if Gertrude Smith was the ringleader, then she would have the loot. That was why she needed a vicious terrier patrolling her property. Then Caitlyn remembered something else: when she and Bertha and the Widow Mags had returned to the cottage, they had met Gertrude coming out, carrying a suitcase. At the time, she had been so preoccupied with Rocco, she hadn't paid much attention, but now it occurred to Caitlyn that Gertrude might have been planning a getaway. With her guard dog gone and Rochat's murder bringing too much police presence, she could've decided to leave her hiding place.

In fact... Caitlyn furrowed her brow as she strained to remember... Gertrude had said: *"first Rochat and the vampire... now this..."* And then later, when Bertha had pressed the cup of tea on her, she had mumbled: *"...need to get out... place is getting too hot..."*

Gertrude hadn't been talking about the weather—she was using the word "hot" as criminal slang for a situation that was too risky for illegal activities.

It all fit. Caitlyn felt a surge of excitement. She couldn't wait to get back and share her suspicions with James: *Gertrude Smith was the ringleader of the Blue Magpies!*

But wait... If she had the loot, surely she wouldn't have risked hiding it in her cottage? Inspector Walsh had even spoken about searching the two cottages. Of course, Gertrude could have refused or insisted on a warrant, but that would have drawn attention. If she was perfectly willing to allow the police inside, the jewels must've been hidden somewhere safe.

But where? Amongst the gardening equipment? No, Caitlyn couldn't see Gertrude stashing millions of pounds worth of jewellery in something like a watering can outside, where it could be lost or damaged... The jewels had to be hidden *in* the cottage. And they had to be easily accessible too, in case Gertrude needed to make a quick getaway—so they couldn't be buried deep under the floorboards or anything like that...

Caitlyn pondered the question all the way back to Huntingdon Manor but was still no nearer an answer when she pulled up in front of the main entrance of the elegant country house. Giles Mosley came hurrying to meet her as she entered the front door.

"Ah, Miss Le Fey—Lord Fitzroy has been worried about you and Miss Sinclair."

Guiltily, Caitlyn realised that they hadn't called to tell James that they would miss lunch. "I'm sorry—we got a bit... um... side-tracked. Anyway, my cousin won't be returning today so it's just me." She glanced around. "Do you know where James and the others are? I'll go and join them."

"Yes, that is why I have been waiting by the front door," said Mosley. "Lord Fitzroy expressly asked me to inform you that they are down at the lake. If you turn left at the Summer Pavilion, next to the rose gardens, and follow the path all the way down, you'll come to the lake. Would you like me to escort you?"

"No, no, I'm sure I can find it, no problems. So did they change their minds about visiting the Folly?"

"I believe they visited the Folly already, straight after lunch."

"Oh." Caitlyn felt guilty again. "I hope me and Pomona being away hasn't messed up the numbers for boating—"

"Not to worry—Lord Fitzroy invited Mrs Smith to join them."

Caitlyn paused. "I'm sorry? Do you mean Gertrude Smith?"

"Yes, she happened to be walking her dog in the rose gardens when the party was on their way to the lake. She seemed pleased to accept Lord Fitzroy's invitation."

"How long ago was that? When did they go down?" asked Caitlyn eagerly.

"About half an hour ago."

"And do you know how long James plans to stay on the lake?"

"I couldn't say, madam. A couple of hours at least, I should think."

Which meant that she probably had an hour's grace before Gertrude Smith and her terrier was likely to return. Caitlyn knew that she really should have called the police and told them her suspicions—let them do a search of the woman's property—but there was no police station in Tillyhenge, and by the time she got hold of Inspector Walsh, explained everything, and convinced him to come, Gertrude would probably be back. No, it was too good an opportunity to miss— she had to seize the chance to search Gertrude's cottage now.

She realised that Giles Mosley was still standing politely next to her and she gave him a quick smile.

"Thanks—I'll head down to the lake now."

Conscious of the butler's eyes on her, Caitlyn walked away as sedately as she could, resisting the urge to break into a run. Once she was out of the Manor, however, she quickened her pace to a jog. She made her way through the rose gardens, pausing by the Summer Pavilion to check that no one was coming up the path from the lake, then turned and headed for the other end, where she found the shortcut path.

A few minutes later, she was outside Gertrude's cottage. She glanced over at Lionel's place next door, wondering if he might be in. She didn't want to have to explain herself if the English teacher saw her breaking into his neighbour's house. But the curtains were drawn and everything seemed quiet next door. She turned back to Gertrude's cottage and considered her options. Obviously, going in through the locked front door was out of the question, but Viktor had got into the kitchen the other day, so perhaps there was a way in the back? Although he had been in his bat form so he could have easily squeezed in through a half-open window...

She walked around the cottage. There was a back door, which probably led into a laundry room next to the kitchen. As she had expected, it was locked and the key wasn't under any of the potted plants nearby. Caitlyn sighed in frustration. Then she remembered a spell she had learnt from Evie—a spell which forced hidden things to reveal themselves. Stretching out her hand towards the door, Caitlyn whispered:

"Manifesto clandestina!"

A large rock tucked next to the back door glowed brightly before fading back to a dull grey. Caitlyn frowned. She had already picked up that rock and checked, and hadn't seen a key underneath. She lifted it again and, as she turned it over, she realised that it wasn't a normal rock—it was a clever replica with a small hollow, a secret compartment where you could hide something. She stuck her fingers in and triumphantly extracted the slim Yale key. A moment later, she was inside the cottage.

CHAPTER TWENTY-FOUR

Quietly, she crept around the tiny property, trying to look for a place where the jewels could have been hidden. She didn't dare disturb things too much, for fear that Gertrude Smith would notice when she returned, and in any case, Caitlyn didn't think that the jewels would be in the obvious hiding places. She paused at last in the kitchen-dining room and stood looking around, her hands on her waist. She sighed again in frustration. Where could the jewels be?

Then something in the corner of the room caught her eye. It was a dog bed and there, tucked in amongst the blankets, was a stuffed toy rabbit. Caitlyn remembered it from the day Viktor had been here, being chased by Rocco the terrier—she had reached to grab the toy, to use it to distract the dog, and Gertrude had yanked it out of her hands. The older woman had claimed that Rocco was possessive of the toy—but now Caitlyn wondered if that was a convenient excuse. Telling everyone that your dog might bite them if they tried to take his toy was a very effective way of keeping their hands off it... and preventing them from discovering that something was hidden inside.

Caitlyn bent down to pick up the toy rabbit and instantly felt the weight of it. No stuffed animal should have been that heavy! Clutching it against her chest, she ran back outside. But once out of the cottage, she paused. Before rushing to the police, she wanted to make sure that the jewels *were* hidden inside. It would be really embarrassing if she turned up at the station, making wild accusations about Gertrude Smith, to then discover that there was nothing more than an artificial weight inserted into the toy. For all she knew, there were dog toys made to be extra heavy for some special reason!

She began turning the toy over, examining it from every angle, but she hadn't had a chance to look properly when something smacked into her from behind, bowling her over.

"Oomph!"

Caitlyn dropped the toy and landed face down on the ground. She rolled over quickly, hands raised in defence—then gave an exasperated laugh as she saw the enormous English mastiff looming over her.

"Bran! You've got to stop bashing into me like that!"

"WOOF!" said the huge dog, wagging his tail. Then he bent his head and picked up the stuffed toy in his cavernous mouth.

"Hey—give me that!" Caitlyn reached for the toy but the dog backed away, his tail wagging excitedly.

"WOOF! WOOF!" said Bran, lumbering around her.

"Bran! Give me that toy!" Caitlyn got to her feet and chased after him.

Mastiffs weren't the fastest of dogs and she caught up with him easily, but getting the toy out of his mouth was another matter. She managed to grab one of the rabbit's furry legs but Bran wouldn't let go. In fact, he seemed to get even more excited as she tried to pull the toy. He jerked his head left and right, and backed away from her, tugging as he went. Caitlyn groaned. He thought it was a game! As far as the mastiff was concerned, they were playing his favourite game of tug-o-war.

"Bran—you've got to let go!" she said desperately, yanking on the toy. "Gertrude Smith is going to come back any minute... I'm running out of time... Let go! LET GO!"

She grasped the toy with both hands and gave a mighty heave. There was a loud *RRRRRRIP!* and she was thrown backwards, landing with a thump that knocked the breath from her. She stared at the tattered remnants of the rabbit's foot she was clutching in one hand. A few feet away, Bran stood facing her, a look of bewilderment on his wrinkled face and half of a soggy stuffed rabbit dangling from his jowly lips. Caitlyn could see dog drool glistening in his mouth.

No, wait a minute. That isn't drool... dog drool doesn't glitter and sparkle like that!

Caitlyn sprang up and ran over. Catching hold of the toy, she begged, "Bran—drop it!"

To her surprise, the mastiff instantly released the toy. Caitlyn shook her head wryly. She had been giving him the wrong command all the time! James must have trained Bran to respond to "drop it", not "let go". Eagerly, she held up the sodden toy and parted the folds of stuffing in the rabbit's abdomen. Her heart leapt as she pulled out a soft fabric bag. The side of it had been torn and now the contents spilled into the palm of her hand.

Caitlyn gasped and stared in wonderment at the glittering stones, and loops of gold and silver.

"Oh my God! Bran, we've found it! We've found it! These are the stolen jewels!"

"WOOF!" said the mastiff, not really understanding but happy and excited anyway. He came over and leaned on her, wagging his tail.

Caitlyn looked back down at the collection in her hands, turning some of the gems over carefully. Yes, there was the pink diamond, so big it looked almost unreal, and of the most beautiful pale salmon colour. It shimmered and sparkled in the sunlight. And then her heart leapt again as she saw something else: an antique silver brooch in the shape of an old-fashioned skeleton key, inlaid with beautiful semi-precious stones, including a large red bloodstone.

Caitlyn extricated it from the pile and held it up to the light. The burnished silver glowed softly and the bloodstone gleamed a vivid red, almost like a drop of blood.

"Ah... *merci beaucoup, mademoiselle*. You have found it for me."

Caitlyn jumped and turned around to see Antoine de Villiers standing behind her. She stared at the handsome Frenchman as he took a step forwards and held out a hand.

"The jewels, if you please?"

Caitlyn barely heard what he said. All she could see was his smile: the dazzling white teeth... and the long fangs that protruded from the corners of his mouth.

CHAPTER TWENTY-FIVE

Caitlyn stood rooted on the spot, her mind spinning. *Antoine? Antoine de Villiers is the vampire?* She couldn't believe it. It was as if her entire world had been tipped upside down. Yes, when they had been following him in London earlier, she had begun to wonder if Pomona was right in thinking that the Frenchman had something to hide, but she had just expected it to be something mundane—an affair with someone's wife, perhaps, or a secret gambling den... Now she stared at him with dawning horror.

"The jewels, *mademoiselle*," he said, his voice becoming impatient. "And do not think of resisting or I may give in to temptation and sink these fangs into your lovely neck." He gave her a mocking smile. "And unlike your friend, Viktor, I am most definitely not a fruitarian. The vampires in my family have always enjoyed the taste of blood."

"But... but you can't be a vampire..." stammered Caitlyn. "Blood makes you feel sick... I saw you... that day in the chocolate shop when Nibs scratched me and there was blood on my arm—"

"I was disturbed, yes, by the sight of your blood, but not because I felt faint and nauseous." He looked amused. "No, on the contrary, it made me hunger and long to taste you myself. But naturally, I could not reveal my true identity. So I fought the urges. It was fortunate that you thought my reaction was due to a squeamish nature." He laughed heartily.

"So that means... you... Pierre Rochat..."

Antoine smiled. "Yes, I killed him. *Imbécile*. He thought he could defy me and he paid dearly. I would have been happy to let him live—it is not my wish to kill and bring attention to my presence—but Rochat sealed his own fate when he intervened. Perhaps he thought he was being gallant in trying to defend the woman..." He laughed humourlessly. "Well, that chivalry cost him his life."

"Woman? You mean Gertrude Smith?" asked Caitlyn, still trying to piece the puzzle together.

"*Oui.* Rochat had arranged to meet her in the woods once the movie had started and everyone was suitably distracted. I observed him stealing away in the darkness—my vampire vision made it easy to track him, even from across the lawn—and I followed him to their meeting place. They were about to make their exchange when I appeared. I asked—most politely, you understand—for the jewels to be given to me, but the woman refused and I was left with no choice but to forcibly take them. Rochat tried to intervene and the rest, as they say, is history."

His face darkened. "However, Rochat's interference did mean that the woman was allowed to escape. Her scream brought too many people to the scene."

"Why didn't you go after Gertrude? She had the jewels."

"The murder investigation... the police around the Manor every day... it was not a good time. I decided it was best to wait. I thought perhaps the woman would expose me but she kept silent. No doubt because she did not wish to reveal her own presence in the forest that night and open herself to police investigation. And perhaps, too, she did not see me clearly in the dark... So, I had intended to wait—*quand tout se sera calmé*—until 'the dust has settled', as they say. In any case, Gertrude Smith had cleverly hidden the jewels and I had not discovered their hiding place..." He smiled. "But you, *mademoiselle*—you have brains as well as beauty, and you have completed the job for me."

He took a step towards her.

"How... how did you know I was here?" Caitlyn asked, desperate to keep him talking.

He looked amused. "I followed you... as you followed me. Ah, you did not think that I noticed you and your cousin behind me on the way to London? But of course I noticed. *C'était très amusant*—I let you have your little game. It did not affect my plans."

"What did you go to London for?"

He laughed again. "You are very inquisitive, *ma cherie*. But surely you do not expect me to divulge all my secrets?"

Caitlyn licked dry lips. "Uh... okay, well... I can take a guess—you went to London to meet someone. Maybe the same person who told you about the stolen jewels in the first place. They told you the ringleader was in Tillyhenge—that's why you invited yourself to Huntingdon Manor, wasn't it?"

"*Bravo*," he said with a chuckle. "*Oui*, I came to seek out the thief who held the jewels. It was serendipitous that I should meet Rochat at the Open-Air Cinema. I knew he was a fence, of course—one becomes familiar with certain names and faces in the jewellery world—and I quickly realised that it must be he who was meeting the thief. I had only to follow him and *voilà*, he would lead me to the jewels."

"But you didn't get the jewels," Caitlyn pointed out. "Is that why you went back to London today—to get your orders from your boss?"

He scowled. "There is no boss. Antoine de Villiers

works for no one but himself! There are those with whom it is beneficial to form a partnership... I get information and, in exchange, I take the necessary action, to achieve a goal which suits both our purposes." He made an impatient sound and held out his hands. "*Assez!* We talk too much. *Tiens...* the jewels, if you please."

Reluctantly, Caitlyn held out her hand and tipped the jewels into his waiting palm. He glanced at them, lifted something out of the pile, and cast the rest aside. The gems tumbled to the ground and lay sparkling amongst the grass and flowers.

Caitlyn stared at Antoine. "But... the pink diamond! You just threw it away!"

"*Bah!* What do I want with diamonds, pink or otherwise? It is *this* that is the real prize."

He held up the antique brooch in the shape of the key. As Caitlyn watched, he carefully detached the pin section from the main part of the brooch, so that all he was holding was the silver key with the inlaid gems and bloodstone.

"It's a real key?" said Caitlyn.

"*Mais oui.* Not 'a key', but *the* key. The key to the belfry."

"But... that's just a legend—"

He laughed harshly. "*Non, non, mademoiselle*— the power of the belfry is very real, as you shall see!" He clamped a hand on her arm. "Come."

"What? No!" Caitlyn tried to pull out of his grasp. "You've... you've got what you wanted now—"

"Ah, but I have not fed in days... and I have been thinking about you, my lovely Caitlyn... The old man, Rochat, may have sustained me for a while but there is nothing like the taste of sweet, innocent blood..."

He leaned towards her and Caitlyn went stiff, her heart pounding with terror. She knew she should try to use magic to defend herself but her mind was blank, her limbs paralysed. Then there came a deep growl next to them. Caitlyn looked down to see the mastiff watching, an uneasy expression on his wrinkled face. Bran was usually the most placid, friendly dog, and Caitlyn knew that he was used to seeing Antoine de Villiers around the Manor, so he would not normally think of the man as a threat. But perhaps Bran sensed her fear. He was clearly disturbed, and an unhappy mastiff was not to be ignored.

Antoine eased himself away from her and pulled something out of his pocket, pointing it at the dog. Caitlyn's heart nearly stopped when she saw that it was a gun.

"NO!" she cried, flinging herself in front of Bran and throwing her arms around his neck.

"As I said, *mademoiselle*, I do not wish to kill if I do not have to. But I will not let the dog interfere with my plans. They have been disrupted too much already." He waved the gun. "Send him away and I will spare him."

Caitlyn crouched next to Bran and pressed her

face close to his, whispering urgently in his ear. "Bran—go get James! Get James, do you hear me? Good boy—go get James!"

She glanced down and saw something glittering next to his front paw. It was an aquamarine pendant. Making sure that her back shielded her from Antoine's gaze, she scooped up the stone and shoved it into the space between the mastiff's neck and his collar. She had no idea if it would remain wedged there, but if it did, and if James saw it, she hoped that it might provide a clue and lead him to her. Then she straightened and gave the mastiff a shove in the direction of the Manor. "Go on, Bran! Good boy—go home!"

The mastiff looked at her uncertainly for a moment, then turned and began lumbering away. Caitlyn had no idea if the dog would be able to raise the alarm, but at least he was safe from Antoine.

"*Bien.* Now, we shall go." Antoine waved the gun mockingly. "After you, *mademoiselle.*"

"Where are we going?"

"I am surprised you need to ask. To the Fitzroy Folly, of course."

CHAPTER TWENTY-SIX

The Folly looked exactly the same as the last time she had visited it. Now that she knew its significance, Caitlyn had expected it to look different somehow—more "magical" perhaps—but it was the same dusty, crumbling tower that she had explored. Antoine waved her ahead and she began to climb the spiralling stone staircase, with him following close behind. Every time she thought about trying to escape, she would feel the prod of the gun muzzle against the small of her back, bite her lip, and continue climbing.

At last, they reached the locked door at the top. Antoine handed her the key.

"Go on—open it."

Caitlyn inserted the silver key and turned it slowly. There was a loud *CLICK* and then the door swung open of its own accord. She stepped through and gasped.

A gigantic black bell hung in the centre of the belfry chamber. Caitlyn stared as a strong wind buffeted her, whipping hair around her face. It was very exposed here, with only open archways and no proper walls around them, and the bell swung slightly in the wind, its black metal surface gleaming dully in the late afternoon sunshine.

"*C'est magnifique, n'est-pas?*" said Antoine, standing next to her. His eyes were burning with a feverish light. "The bell of the legend... the bell to call up a great army... and a chance for my kind to be great again!" He laughed wildly. "No more do we wait in vain for the Fates to decide when the next vampire child will be born. No, with this, I shall have the power to create vampires—an entire army of them!"

Caitlyn shook her head and pleaded with him: "Antoine, this is wrong! You know this is wrong! You shouldn't meddle with what nature intended—"

"You speak like all the old vampires," said Antoine contemptuously. "They are weak and defeated and resigned... *Non*, I refuse to be like that. I refuse to accept the old way as the only way. It is time for a new approach, a new way of doing things. Why do you look so angry, *ma cherie*? My friend, James—whom you so admire—he thinks the way I do."

"James is nothing like you! He would never do

anything that would hurt others. This... this vampire army that you're creating—you would also be unleashing a plague on mankind. Surely you don't want that?"

Antoine gave a cold laugh. "What do I care about mankind? They are weak and inept. They do not deserve to be saved... well, except perhaps for those such as yourself," he said with a smirk, looking at her in a way that made her skin crawl. "I would keep a small harem, perhaps, of human girls to amuse me... Mm... your beautiful cousin, Pomona— she would be a great addition too... I sense her dislike of me and I would enjoy... taming her..."

Caitlyn felt a surge of anger at his cruelty, his callousness, his smug arrogance... She couldn't let Antoine achieve his plans! She looked around wildly and spotted a large black mallet lying beneath the bell. She knew instinctively that it was needed to strike the bell—to call the army of bats.

She broke away from Antoine and ran towards the mallet, snatching it up and racing to the other side of the belfry. There, she braced herself against one of the stone archways and flung it out as far as she could. It sailed through the air and disappeared into the forest canopy below. She knew it might not stop Antoine permanently, but it would at least slow him down—he wouldn't be able to use the bell until he found the mallet again, and it would take him time to find it in the dense undergrowth of the woods.

"*Diable!*" growled Antoine, rushing up beside her and staring down at where the mallet had disappeared. "You little witch! You shall pay for that!" He turned furiously and seized her, yanking her towards him.

She screamed. From far below them, she heard a faint echoing cry:

"Caitlyn!"

It was James's voice. She twisted her head and looked over her shoulder, catching a glimpse of the ground below. Two men were running out of the woods and hurrying towards the tower. The first was James and the second, hobbling as fast as he could behind the younger man, was Viktor. The two men were accompanied by Bran the mastiff, who barked furiously as he ran around the base of the tower.

Antoine swore again; then he laughed. "They will not save you, *cherie*—with all those steps, by the time James gets to the top of the tower, it will be too late..." He lifted his lips, baring his fangs, and lunged towards her.

Caitlyn screamed and jerked out of the way. She managed to wriggle sideways, but found herself wedged against the side of the belfry chamber. There was nothing behind her but the stone ledge and, beyond that, the sheer drop to the ground below.

Antoine lunged again, grabbing her arms and pinning them to her sides as he lowered his head towards her neck. Caitlyn struggled wildly, screaming and crying for help, and flung herself backwards in her terror. Her sudden move unbalanced Antoine and he fell on top of her. They teetered for a moment on the ledge, then toppled over the side.

"*Nooo!*" Caitlyn gasped, clawing at the stones around her.

She heard Antoine curse as he, too, tried desperately to find a handhold, then a wild cry came from him as he slipped and went over. Caitlyn shrieked as she felt him dragging her with him.

She was falling... falling...!

"Unggh!"

Caitlyn jerked to a stop. She had managed to catch the ledge with her right hand, and now she hung on, sobbing with fear. She was lopsided, her legs dangling in the air. She flailed desperately with her left arm, trying to swing it up and catch the ledge as well, but she just couldn't reach.

She choked back tears of terror. Her right arm was starting to shake, the muscles beginning to spasm as she struggled to support her weight. The fingers of her right hand were going numb and she could feel them slipping on the stone. She knew that she wouldn't be able to hold on much longer...

Then something caught hold of her collar and lifted her upwards, helping to prop her up in the air and ease the weight on her arm. Caitlyn gasped and looked up to see a fuzzy brown fruit bat hovering in the air above her head.

Viktor!

He was beating his wings furiously and his clawed feet were clenched in the fabric of her shirt, yanking it up. There was a large tear in one wing, making his flight crooked, but he still flapped his wings valiantly, doing his best to hold her in the air. Caitlyn felt a rush of relief and gratitude. She turned back to the stone wall of the tower and tried once again to stretch her left hand up and reach the ledge. With Viktor taking some of her weight, she managed to heave her left arm up and...

Yes! She caught the edge of the stone with her fingers. Feeling a surge of hope, she clung on now with two hands and tried to find a foothold so she could climb up. But the tower was too smooth. She almost lost her hold again when her foot slipped. She gave up and hoped desperately that James would reach the top soon.

The fruit bat was starting to make frantic squeaking noises and Caitlyn realised that it was tiring. It wasn't strong enough to bear her weight for long, especially with that damaged wing. Already, she was sinking lower and lower as the exhausted bat grew weaker. She looked desperately up at the ledge again. Without a foothold, the only way she could haul herself back up was if she could do a pull-up, using just her arms. But she was clinging to the ledge by the tips of her fingers and barely had the upper-body strength to hang on, never mind haul herself up...

"Caitlyn!"

Suddenly, two strong hands gripped her wrists. It was James. He was there, panting heavily, his face a mixture of relief and terror. The next moment, Caitlyn felt herself being pulled to safety.

"Caitlyn... oh my God, Caitlyn..."

James caught her in his arms and hugged her close, dropping his cheek against her forehead. Caitlyn clung to him, trembling, and savoured the feel of his warm body against hers, his strong arms around her. She had never felt so safe, so cherished as at that moment. She could feel James's heart pounding against hers and she realised suddenly how terrified he had been.

"James..." she choked, wanting to say something but still unable to talk.

"Shh... It's all right... you're safe now..." he said, stroking her hair tenderly with one hand.

Caitlyn felt his lips brush her temple, then linger against her ear and down the side of her jaw. She raised her face, her heart hammering—although whether it was still from fear or something else, she didn't know—and looked up into James's dark grey eyes. His lips were inches away from hers and Caitlyn felt herself trembling with anticipation.

Slowly, his arms tightened around her... he lowered his head towards hers...

A burst of high-pitched squeaks sounded suddenly next to them, breaking them apart. A little brown fruit bat reeled up from the side of the tower and lurched over their heads, flapping weakly as the strong wind buffeted him one way, then the other. Then he fell in a tangle of leathery wings to hit the side of the bell and land on the floor of the belfry with a thump.

"Oh!" cried Caitlyn, breaking free from James's embrace and running over to the bat. She scooped up the little creature and cradled it in her arms. Thankfully, it didn't look like it was seriously hurt, just slightly stunned. Already, it was making grumpy squeaks and struggling to stand up.

"Is it all right?" asked James, coming up behind her. He peered down at the furry creature. "That was the bat that was trying to save you! It was the most extraordinary thing. I mean, I've heard of altruistic behaviour in animals—there are lots of cases of dolphins rescuing people—but I've never heard of it in small animals." He shook his head. "Perhaps it mistook you for prey or something—but it really did look like it was trying to hold you up and stop you falling."

Caitlyn hid a smile and looked down at the fruit bat. "Perhaps I've got a little guardian angel."

CHAPTER TWENTY-SEVEN

"I still can't believe that the murderer wasn't that English teacher after all!" Beth Jenkins shook her head incredulously.

"You sure now?" asked Jeremy Bottom, scratching his head.

Caitlyn nodded. They were standing together on the edge of the village green, next to the pub. It was a lovely summer's morning and she couldn't believe that only a day ago, she had been hanging from the top of the Folly, fighting for her life.

"Who's the murderer?"

They all looked down to see Molly standing next to her mother, listening wide-eyed.

"Nobody, darling!" said Beth hastily. She gestured to the cat carrier that Caitlyn was holding. "Why don't you take Nibs over to that bench there and have a play with him, while Mummy has a little chat?"

"Okay," said Molly, holding out her pudgy hands for the wicker cage.

"Be careful—don't let him out of the carrier," Caitlyn told the little girl as she passed the kitten over. "I need to take him up to the Manor and I don't want him to run off."

The little girl toddled off with the kitten and Beth turned back to Caitlyn. She lowered her voice and said, "So the police have *definitely* ruled out the English teacher?"

"Yes," Caitlyn said. "It definitely isn't Lionel Spelling."

"But I heard that he was seen sneaking off into the woods on the night of the murder. Old Palmer was telling everyone in the pub yesterday that he saw him... but that day in the chocolate shop, Lionel Spelling said he never left his cottage. That means that he was lying, doesn't it?"

Caitlyn marvelled at the woman's memory. "Yes, you're right. He was lying—but not because he murdered anyone. The police questioned him again last night and he broke down and confessed: he's been illegally distilling liquor. He makes up a few batches during the holiday breaks and sells them to his students when he gets back to the language school. He's got a home-made still hidden in the woods and he was going to check on it that night. But of course, he didn't want to admit that to the police."

"That slimy git was making moonshine in the woods? I told you he was up to no good!" said Jeremy triumphantly.

Beth frowned. "Yes, but if Lionel Spelling didn't murder that man, then who did?"

"Er..." Caitlyn hesitated. A sense of loyalty to James made her reluctant to badmouth his friend. "Well, the police have a good idea who it is but they haven't apprehended him yet."

Which was the truth. When they had finally come back down to the bottom of the Folly yesterday, Caitlyn had expected to find Antoine's lifeless body sprawled at the base of the tower. Instead, there was nothing—not a trace of the man. Caitlyn had been bewildered until she remembered that Antoine de Villiers was a vampire. Just like Viktor, he could shift into a bat at will—so it would have been the first thing he did when he found himself free-falling from the tower. He must have transformed and flown away to safety.

Now, she gave Beth a conspiratorial smile and said, "I think they're keeping his identity confidential for the moment, but I'm sure you'll hear as soon as he's arrested."

"Well, do you know if the murderer *was* the ringleader of the jewel thieves?" asked Beth, obviously hoping to squeeze out every last bit of information for the village gossip mill. "Isn't that what they said—that Pierre Rochat was a fence and

257

came to Tillyhenge to meet the thieves and get the jewels?"

"Yes, he *did* come to Tillyhenge to do a deal—he planned to meet the ringleader during the movie. But the murderer wanted the jewels too and tried to interrupt the exchange. Pierre Rochat resisted and he got killed in the struggle."

Jeremy whistled. "So they were two different people? Everyone thought the ringleader and the murderer were the same person."

Caitlyn nodded. "That's what I thought too at first. I never thought there were three people in the woods that night: Rochat, the ringleader of the thieves, and the murderer."

Beth frowned. "So who is the ringleader then? Have the police at least arrested *him*?"

"It's a 'her', actually—the ringleader is Gertrude Smith," Caitlyn said.

"*Gertrude Smith*?" Beth's voice rose several octaves.

Caitlyn nodded. "That's not even her name. Her real name is Geertje Smidt and she's a Dutch criminal who's been on Interpol's list for decades."

"But she... but she..." Beth spluttered. "She looked so respectable—"

"That was just a clever disguise. And it obviously worked if you never even suspected her," said Caitlyn with a wry smile.

"Oh, *I* always suspected her... always thought there was something fishy about that woman!

Thought it was drugs, of course... It could have been too—the Dutch think doing the recreational stuff is okay, don't they? But I knew there was something off. I told my missus, there's something fishy about that woman..."

They turned to see Terry the pub landlord coming out of his establishment to join them. Caitlyn's eyes widened as she saw who was trotting at Terry's heels: Rocco the terrier! The little dog followed the landlord down the steps in front of the pub, then froze, his nose twitching. He jerked his head across to the nearby bench where Molly was sitting. Caitlyn's heart sank as she saw that the little girl had disobeyed her: Molly had lifted Nibs out of the carrier and was now sitting with the kitten on her lap.

Caitlyn called urgently, "Molly! Put Nibs back—"

It was too late. The terrier had seen the kitten. He rushed towards the bench, barking and snarling, just as Molly looked up and squealed with fright. The kitten on her lap puffed up into a little ball of spiky black fur and then, to Caitlyn's astonishment, launched himself, hissing and spitting, at the approaching dog.

The terrier skidded to a stop, an almost comical expression of shock and confusion on his face. There was a flash of claws and a howl of pain, and the next moment, Rocco had turned tail and was trying to get away from Nibs as fast as he could.

Caitlyn burst out laughing. The last thing she

had expected was to see the ferocious terrier bested by a little kitten! Nibs gave a last hiss, then turned and stalked back to Molly, his tiny bottle-brush tail straight up in the air.

"Here now!" said Terry, looking down at the cowering dog as Beth and Jeremy laughed too. "What's that all about? Can't believe he's scared of a wee kitten. The police told me he was a vicious brute when they tried to get in the cottage yesterday without his owner there. That's why I decided to take him."

"You're adopting Rocco?" said Caitlyn in surprise.

"Yes, been thinking about getting a guard dog for the pub and the police said the poor tyke needed a home, now that his owner's been arrested... So I offered to take him in." He bent to pat the dog, who seemed to recover a bit and wag his tail. "He's a good size—and very smart. Reckon he could even be trained as a drug-sniffer dog," said Terry proudly.

Oh dear, Caitlyn thought as she eyed the small dog warily. With Rocco taking up residence at the pub, poor Bran was going to be harassed by the terrier every time he came into the village. Still... She glanced over to the bench where Nibs was back in Molly's lap and smiled to herself. *Maybe Bran will be fine as long as he's got Nibs with him for protection!*

"By the way, where's your cousin... Pomona, isn't it?" asked Beth. "Wasn't she staying with you at the

Manor?"

"Er... yes, she was, but she's... um... gone up to London," Caitlyn said, trying to dredge up a bright smile.

She didn't add that—aside from a couple of brief texts—she hadn't heard from Pomona since they had parted at Harrods. She had tried to call her cousin this morning but hadn't managed to get through, and she didn't feel that her harrowing experience in the Folly was something she wanted to explain via text messages. Still, she was hoping to hear back from Pomona later that day... and she was trying not to worry. After all, as Pomona had said herself, she was a big girl now and had been taking care of herself for years. There must have been countless late nights and wild parties back in L.A. that Caitlyn had never known about—so why should this be any different? Resolutely, Caitlyn thrust the image of the dark-haired man with the piercing blue eyes out of her mind and turned back to Beth.

"Well, I'd better get on," she said. "I've got to take Nibs up to the Manor."

"How's that going then?" asked Beth with coy glance. "I heard that you and Lord Fitzroy are sharing the kitten? What an unusual arrangement!"

"Yes, well, we rescued him together... er, I mean, we happened to be together when we found him... I mean, not 'together' like a couple or anything... Just, um... I was walking up near the stone circle and met James out walking Bran... Anyway, we both heard the kitten crying and we found him in the abandoned quarry pool in the woods. He had fallen in and would have drowned if we hadn't rescued him."

"What a romantic story!" said Beth, holding a hand to her heart. "So now you're 'sharing' him?"

"Actually, Nibs was going to live at the Manor—it's really the better place for him—but he kept trying to stow away with me every time I came back to the chocolate shop," said Caitlyn with a laugh. "And the Widow Mags loves having him around. So James and I worked out this arrangement where Nibs would live with me part of the week and live at the Manor the rest of the time."

"Ah... well, Nibs might find himself living at the Manor full-time before long..." said Beth with a meaningful smile.

Caitlyn felt herself blushing and looked quickly away. She knew that the villagers loved to gossip about her and they constantly wondered about her relationship with their handsome "lord of the manor". After all, she was a complete stranger who had arrived in the village from overseas and was often seen in the company of James Fitzroy, who was probably one of the most eligible bachelors in England...

Any female around James would have been the subject of much speculation, never mind one surrounded by as much mystery as she was!

CHAPTER TWENTY-EIGHT

The villagers aren't the only ones wondering what's going on between James and me, thought Caitlyn as she drove up the driveway of Huntingdon Manor. She flashed back to that moment at the top of the tower, when James had held her in his arms... had he been going to kiss her? Or had it just been the heightened emotions of the moment? Sighing, Caitlyn parked her car, got out, and lifted Nibs in his carrier.

"*Meew!*" cried the kitten, looking eagerly around.

"All right—here you go," said Caitlyn, setting the wicker carrier down on the front steps of the Manor and opening the cage door.

The kitten scampered out, mewing loudly. A moment later, there came an answering bark and an English mastiff appeared from around the side of the Manor. He lumbered up to Nibs and touched noses with the kitten.

"Hi Bran," said Caitlyn, smiling and reaching out to pat the huge head. "I haven't even thanked you properly for saving my life. If you hadn't got James to come to the tower—"

"It's the one time I'm glad he ignored his training," said James, appearing from the side of the Manor after Bran. He came up to Caitlyn and gave her a twisted smile. "We were just about to go for another round on the boats when Bran arrived and started barking at me. I kept telling him to be quiet and go away, but he wouldn't listen—which was very unlike him. Then I saw that aquamarine pendant tucked in his collar and I realised that something was wrong."

"Oh, I'm so glad you saw that!" said Caitlyn. "I didn't know if it would work but it was the only thing I could think of at the time."

"It worked, all right—although I wouldn't have known where to find you if Bran hadn't picked up your scent and led me straight to the Folly." James looked at her, the horror of that moment still vivid in his grey eyes. "When I think about what might have happened if I'd had to waste time searching for you in the forest and didn't get to the Folly in time—"

"But you did," said Caitlyn quickly. "And I'm here now, safe and sound... so all's well that ends well."

"What happened to that little bat?" James asked.

"I still think you should have let me take him to the vet. Russell is very good and his clinic would have looked after the bat while it was recovering—"

"Oh, he's—I mean, it's fine," said Caitlyn, thinking that Viktor would have never forgiven her if she had let him fall into the hands of the veterinarian again! "I... um... gave the bat to Bertha to look after. She's very good with animals and she's got some herbal tonics which help them recover really quickly."

Actually, the last time she'd seen Viktor was that morning, when she found him and the Widow Mags in the kitchen of *Bewitched by Chocolate*, arguing like an old married couple about the best berries for fruitcake. His arm had been almost healed and he had seemed completely recovered from his ordeal.

"And you?" asked James. "Are you feeling all right?"

"Yes, fine," Caitlyn assured him. "The paramedics said I didn't even pull a muscle in my arm. I was very lucky."

He frowned. "I still don't understand what happened. You weren't very clear when Inspector Walsh questioned you yesterday. What were you and Antoine doing up in the Folly?" His gaze hardened. "I couldn't see very well from the bottom of the tower but it looked like the two of you were struggling. You were screaming. Was he trying to harm you?"

Caitlyn licked her lips, wondering whether to tell

him the truth: *"Yes, your friend is a vampire and he was trying to kill me."* What would James do if he heard that? He would never believe her. It was easier just to fib and tell a version of the truth.

"He... um... I think Antoine wanted to kiss me..." she said, looking down and twisting her hands. "And I didn't want him to... So he was... um... trying to force himself on me..."

"The bastard."

Caitlyn looked up, shocked. James looked furious. Her heart leapt. Maybe he did care...?

James clenched his fists. "If he hadn't disappeared, I would have thrashed him myself."

"Have... have the police found him yet?"

"No. There's no sign of him. His things were gone from the Manor too." James shook his head. "The whole thing just doesn't make sense! I can't believe that Antoine was the murderer. Why would he kill Pierre Rochat? For some jewels? His family is one of the wealthiest in France—he wouldn't need to kill to obtain jewels! He regularly patronises several luxury jewellery stores. In any case, they were all just tossed on the ground—even the pink diamond. If he killed Rochat for the jewels, why didn't he take them, then?" He looked keenly at Caitlyn. "Did he say anything to you?"

"N-no, not really," Caitlyn said, shifting uncomfortably. "I mean, like I told Inspector Walsh, he came up to me just as I discovered the jewels hidden in the dog toy, and he confessed to killing

Rochat for them."

"But then he just walked off with you and left them lying there on the grass?"

Caitlyn swallowed. James was no fool and she should have known that he wouldn't easily accept the explanation that she had given to the police. She shrugged helplessly.

"I... I don't know." Then hurriedly, to get his mind off Antoine, she asked, "Has Gertrude Smith talked?"

"Yes, she finally broke down this morning," said James. "I just got off the phone with Inspector Walsh, actually. She admitted that her gang, the Blue Magpies, stole the jewels from the boutique in Mayfair and that she had arranged to meet Pierre Rochat in Tillyhenge to discuss their sale. Apparently, he had a buyer lined up for the pink diamond already. Or at least, part of the pink diamond. It's common practice for jewel thieves to cut up a bigger stone, to make it less recognisable and easier to dispose of."

"Wow. I'll bet the owner is glad that didn't happen!"

"Yes, he's very grateful to get his collection back—well, all of the pieces except for an antique brooch." James frowned. "In fact, this seems to be the brooch that you were asking Inspector Walsh about—you know, the one with the embedded bloodstone. The police couldn't find it amongst the pieces they retrieved outside Gertrude's cottage. Did you see it when you opened the dog toy?"

Caitlyn hesitated. She knew where the brooch was—or at least, the key part of the brooch. It was safely concealed now in the Widow Mags's bedroom and nobody else knew of its hiding place except her, Bertha, and Viktor.

"Um... I wasn't really looking properly," she said at last. She hated having to lie to James but there seemed to be no other way.

James sighed. "I know it may sound silly but I feel partly responsible as this all happened on my estate. I spoke to the owner earlier today and he is very upset about the loss."

"But the brooch isn't very valuable, is it? Not like the pink diamond?"

"It's not worth much but it does have a lot of sentimental value. He found it in a chest belonging to his grandmother. They'd lost most of her things in a fire and only just recently discovered this chest in the attic—he was delighted to have found something of hers. The police have said that they are going to keep searching, but somehow I have a feeling that it will remain a mystery." James gave her a wry look. "The place seems to be brimming with mysteries lately. Inspector Walsh told me that when the police searched the Folly, they found no evidence of a bell in the belfry chamber. It was empty, just like when I saw it as a boy. And yet... I could have *sworn* that there was a large black bell hanging in the centre when I rushed in to save you!

You saw it, didn't you?"

Again, Caitlyn was torn over how to answer. She wished she could explain the truth to James: tell him that when the key had been withdrawn from the lock, the enchantment over the Folly had been broken and the huge black bell had vanished, leaving nothing but an empty belfry behind. But once again, she didn't think he would believe her. He might even think that she was crazy. She remembered what Pomona had told her about James's girlfriend at university; if Caitlyn started talking about spells and enchantments, would he recoil from her too?

No, she couldn't risk it. If it was possible that James Fitzroy might care for her, she didn't want to lose that—his respect and affection—by telling him the truth about magic and witchcraft. Maybe one day... maybe one day she could try to make him understand... but in the meantime, it was a secret she had to keep to herself.

"I... um... I wasn't paying much attention, to tell you the truth. I was just trying to get away from Antoine. Anyway," she said, giving him a bright smile, "I think we both want to forget every moment of what happened in the tower yesterday."

James looked at her silently, his eyes very dark. "Not *every* moment," he finally said.

Caitlyn stared up at him, her heart pounding. Could he have meant what she thought?

James cleared his throat, then took a step closer.

"Caitlyn... you know that I... well, I'm not very good at expressing how I feel..." He gave a self-deprecating laugh, then cleared his throat again. "I may not shower you with compliments... like some other men do... but I hope you know how much you mean to me. When I saw you at the top of the Folly and I thought you were going to fall..." He swallowed convulsively. "I couldn't bear to lose—"

The front door of the Manor opened and Giles Mosley stepped out.

"Sir, I'm sorry to interrupt but your sister is on the phone."

James cursed under his breath. "Can you tell her I'll call her back?"

"She says it's urgent, sir."

James sighed, then he nodded at the butler. "Thank you, Mosley—I'll be right there."

The butler disappeared into the house and James turned back to Caitlyn.

"Caitlyn... Look, don't go away, okay? I'll be back as soon as I can." He gave her brief smile, then hurried inside.

Caitlyn realised that she was standing with a silly grin on her face and hastily wiped it off. She took a deep breath, then let it out slowly. Was this it? Would she find out at last what James really felt for her? She thought of the expression in his soft grey eyes when he'd looked at her just now, and a mixture of hope and nervous anticipation filled her breast.

Then something flitting above her head caught her attention. She looked up and shaded her eyes. Was it a large insect? No, wait... it was the Widow Mags's runaway spectacles!

Caitlyn jumped up to grab the flying glasses, her fingers just missing them as they darted out of the way. They had obviously learnt new tricks in the wild because they did a few fancy loops in mid-air before zooming in a figure of eight around her head.

"Oh no you don't!" cried Caitlyn, lunging again to grab them. This time, she managed to catch hold of one side of the frame and she hung on as the spectacles struggled to get free.

"You've had your fun—now it's time to go home to the Widow Mags," she said sternly. She screwed up her face, trying to remember the spell that Evie had used, then pointed a finger at the wriggling spectacles and chanted:

"Gravity obey,
To earth you must stay!"

There was a crackling sound and something sparked from the ends of her fingers. The flying spectacles glowed suddenly like a burning ember, then faded back to their original colour. They went limp in her hands, becoming nothing more than an ordinary pair of reading glasses.

Caitlyn laughed with delight. "Hah! I did it!"

A sound behind her made her whirl around.

Her stomach clenched as she saw James standing at the top of the Manor's front steps. She didn't know how long he had been there, but from the expression on his face, it was clear he had seen everything. His eyes met hers and Caitlyn flinched at the shock and horror in them.

"What... what was that?" he asked, his voice strained. He came slowly down the steps and stared at her. There was a long silence, then he said at last:

"Who *are* you?"

FINIS

Don't miss your next wickedly delicious chocolate fix!

Book 5 *in the*
BEWITCHED BY CHOCOLATE Mysteries

COMING SOON!

Sign up to my newsletter to be notified when it is released! Go to: **www.hyhanna.com/newsletter**

BEWITCHED BY CHOCOLATE MYSTERIES

Dark, Witch & Creamy (Book 1)

Witch Chocolate Fudge (Book 2)

Witch Summer Night's Cream (Book 3)

Witch Chocolate Bites (Book 4)

~ more coming soon!

**For other books by H.Y. Hanna,
please visit her website:
www.hyhanna.com**

ABOUT THE AUTHOR

H.Y. Hanna is an award-winning mystery and suspense writer and the author of the bestselling *Oxford Tearoom Mysteries*. She has also written romantic suspense and sweet romance, as well as a children's middle-grade mystery series. After graduating from Oxford University with a BA in Biological Sciences and a MSt in Social Anthropology, Hsin-Yi tried her hand at a variety of jobs, before returning to her first love: writing.

She worked as a freelance journalist for several years, with articles and short stories published in the UK, Australia and NZ, and has won awards for her novels, poetry, short stories and journalism.

A globe-trotter all her life, Hsin-Yi has lived in a variety of cultures, from Dubai to Auckland, London to New Jersey, but is now happily settled in Perth, Western Australia, with her husband and a rescue kitty named Muesli. You can learn more about her (and the real-life Muesli who inspired the cat character in the story) and her other books at: **www.hyhanna.com**.

Sign up to her newsletter to be notified of new releases, exclusive giveaways and other book news! Go to: **www.hyhanna.com/newsletter**

ACKNOWLEDGMENTS

I am always so grateful to my beta readers: Connie Leap, Basma Alwesh and Melanie G. Howe, for making time in their busy lives to read the first draft and give me such helpful and insightful feedback. My thanks also to my editor and proofreader for being such a great team to work with.

And to my wonderful husband, for his constant support and encouragetment – for always listening, always cheering me on and always believing in me.

52851230R00173

Made in the USA
San Bernardino, CA
30 August 2017